WITHDRAWN

Impossible Things

Impossible Things

J
STE

Robin Stevenson

ORCA BOOK PUBLISHERS

Library and Archives Canada Cataloguing in Publication

Stevenson, Robin H. (Robin Hjørdis), 1968-
Impossible things / written by Robin Stevenson.

ISBN 978-1-55143-736-1

I. Title.

PS8637.T487I56 2008   jC813'.6   C2007-907381-6

First published in the United States, 2008

Library of Congress Control Number: 2007942243

Summary: Cassidy thinks that making friends is impossible until she meets Victoria, who has some very unusual abilities.

Orca Book Publishers gratefully acknowledges the support for its publishing programs provided by the following agencies: the Government of Canada through the Book Publishing Industry Development Program and the Canada Council for the Arts, and the Province of British Columbia through the BC Arts Council and the Book Publishing Tax Credit.

Cover and text design by Teresa Bubela
Cover artwork by Getty Images

ORCA BOOK PUBLISHERS	ORCA BOOK PUBLISHERS
PO Box 5626, STN. B	PO Box 468
VICTORIA, BC CANADA	CUSTER, WA USA
V8R 6S4	98240-0468

www.orcabook.com
Printed and bound in Canada.

11 10 09 08 • 4 3 2 1

To Kai, with all my love.

Acknowledgments

Many thanks to Cheryl, Ilse and Giles for their endless support; to Bird, the first kid to read it, for her enthusiasm; and to all the friends who cheered me on when I decided to write a book and who celebrated every step of the journey with me. I am very grateful to Pat Schmatz and Gwynneth Evans, for their encouragement and insightful suggestions, and to my editor, Sarah Harvey, for her consistently thoughtful advice and guidance.

One

I probably wouldn't have paid much attention to the new kid if Amber and Madeline hadn't decided to make her their next victim. I stood in the hallway and watched as they stared at her from about two feet away, snickering and pointing. Short brown hair, glasses and blue jeans. She couldn't have looked more ordinary if she'd tried. I balled my hands into tight fists and took a deep breath. Maybe the new kid and I had nothing in common but our enemies, but I might as well show her that the environment at school wasn't totally hostile.

I walked over and nodded at her, ignoring the other girls completely. "Hey, welcome to Parkside. It's kind of like a reality show, you know?"

She looked blank.

"Um, like *Survivor*? Once these two establish their place at the top of the food chain and vote you off the island, things may improve." I glanced toward Amber and Madeline. "Or not. In my experience, not."

The new girl stared at me, eyes wide behind the dark frames of her glasses, her mouth slightly open.

"Oh, social advice from Thrift Store Cassidy," Amber sneered, deliberately lisping my name. *Cathidy*. She planted her hands on her hips and gave the new girl a long hard look. "You ought to watch who you get friendly with. Hanging out with the school freak…"

Madeline nodded. "Social suicide."

The new girl didn't say anything. I grinned at her; then I turned to the other two and made a gurgling noise in my throat. Unlike the rest of my family, I don't have any amazing talents, but I am pretty good at noises. I gurgled a bit more and then I laughed at the disgusted expressions on their faces. "How many times do I have to flush before you go away?" I asked.

There was a muffled snort from beside me: the new girl choking back a laugh.

Amber narrowed her eyes. "Well, I guess you've made your choice then," she told the new girl coldly. "Come on, Maddy. Let's go." She linked her arm through her friend's and they sauntered off down the hallway.

I watched them go, my relief mixed with guilt. I hadn't meant to, but I'd probably just made everything harder for the new girl. "Look, I'm sorry," I told her. "I'll go. If you just ignore me or better yet, shout a few insults at lunchtime, they'll forget that you laughed. They're always eager for more followers."

She held out her hand. No one shakes hands in the seventh grade. It was like something my brother would do—in other words, not entirely normal. I grinned and took her hand. "Cassidy Silver."

"Victoria Morris." She watched me for a moment, gray-blue eyes thoughtful behind the glasses, her lips curved in a hint of a smile. "How come they called you that?"

"Thrift Store Cassidy?" I looked down at my outfit: a green T-shirt that read *Humpty Dumpty Was Pushed*, a multicolored silk scarf and a pair of faded jeans with patched knees. "Isn't it obvious?"

Her cheeks flushed. "Not your clothes. I meant, why did they call you Cathidy?"

Because they know I hate it. That would've been the honest answer, but I didn't like to admit that it bothered me. "I used to lisp," I said carefully, making sure I didn't. Years of speech therapy and still, if I was stressed or not concentrating, the lisp would sneak back.

"Oh. That's…that's so mean."

"Um, yeah. Mean is what they do best." I looked at her curiously. "Wasn't it like this at your old school? Where'd you go before this anyway? Did you just move here or something?"

She nodded. "Yes, we moved." Her eyes slid away from mine for a moment; then she looked right at me and smiled again. A full-on smile this time—two rows of small white teeth and lots of pink gums. "You're in grade seven too? What's our teacher like?"

"Ah. Well, I'm afraid he's not quite human." I sucked my bottom lip between my teeth, making a long, drawn-out, squeaking noise. "No description will do him justice. You'll see." I glanced at my watch and picked up the battered briefcase I lug my school stuff around in. "Come on. If we're late, he'll eat us alive."

The seventh grade classroom was kind of like a large jail cell, minus the bunk and toilet. Mr. McMaran had taken down all the artwork on the first day. He said he didn't want us staring at pictures when we were supposed to be working. The fluorescent ceiling lights hummed overhead. It was sunny outside, a bright January day, but the blinds were tightly closed. I sighed, made a face at Victoria and took my seat in the back row. I liked to sit near the door. It gave me the illusion that I could escape if necessary.

"Welcome to the jungle," I whispered, patting the desk beside mine. "Sit here. It's a good spot for those of us low on the food chain."

Victoria gave that muffled snort of a laugh again and sat down at the empty desk.

"Seriously. From back here you can watch Amber and Madeline tossing their ponytails, giggling and passing notes." I gestured to the front of the room, waving my hand like I was a tour guide. "And to our left? The outsiders." With a sweep of my arm, I took in quiet nervous Nathan

Cressman with his smooth black skin and too-big glasses and too-small pants, half asleep with his head on his folded arms; dark-eyed Joe Cicarelli, always in trouble; and chubby Felicia Morgan. I nodded my head toward her. "See the dark-haired girl there? Definitely voted off the island."

The door banged open. Mr. McMaran stomped in and slammed it behind him. "Get out your history texts," he said. "Start reading where we left off."

Apparently he wasn't much in the mood for teaching. He grunted a few instructions; then he sat at his desk and read a glossy magazine about cigars. I snuck another sideways peek at Victoria. I wondered how long it would be before she realized that hanging around with me really was social suicide. I wondered how much longer it would be before she decided to cut her losses and move on. And I wondered how much longer I could go on pretending I didn't care that I had no friends.

Two

If it had been up to me, I'd have hit the road running as soon as the bell rang, but Mom made me wait for Ben. Ben, she claimed, was too young to walk home alone. Personally I thought Ben was more than capable. He wasn't exactly your average eight-year-old.

Mom wouldn't listen to me though. She didn't have the time. So I waited for Ben, like I did every single day. I refused to spend an extra minute in the school, so I waited outside, at the bottom of the stone stairs.

I was still standing there when Amber and Madeline came marching down. "Waiting for your little brother?" Amber cooed.

I ignored her. I was all out of smart comebacks. She just shrugged and walked away with Madeline, both of them giggling. I shuffled my feet and banged them on the icy pavement. My toes were freezing.

Ben came running around the corner so fast he almost flew right past me.

"Hey!" I grabbed his jacket sleeve. "Whoa! What's the rush?"

He was breathing hard and his face was flushed. "Come on, Cassidy. Let's go."

"What's wrong?"

Ben's wool hat had slipped down his forehead, covering his eyebrows and the top half of his glasses. He squinted up at me. "Nothing, but let's get out of here, okay?" His words came out in a rush, tripping over each other.

"Are those kids bothering you again? Look, maybe you should tell Mom."

"I already did."

"And?"

He sighed. "And she says they have low self-esteem and I should just ignore them."

I rolled my eyes. "You want me to talk to them?"

"No!" He shook his head. "I'm fine."

"Okay then." Not like I really wanted a confrontation with Tyler Patterson and his little fourth-grade gang.

Ben walked along silently, kicking at chunks of ice. He didn't seem fine, but I didn't bother saying anything. He wouldn't talk to me about it until he decided he wanted to. Anyway, I already knew what the problem was. Ben might be smarter than Tyler and his friends when it came to reading and math and memorizing bizarre trivia, but he was a year younger, a whole lot smaller and a bit clueless about trying to fit in. Besides, Tyler was

Amber's younger brother; and apparently bullying ran in the family.

"You can't let them walk all over you," I told him. "You can't make them like you, but you don't have to let them bully you."

"Right," he said sullenly. "Like I should take advice on my social life from you. You're half the reason I get picked on."

I felt like he'd just punched me in the stomach. "What—what do you mean?" As soon as the words were out of my mouth, I wished I could reach up and snatch them back. I didn't want to hear the answer.

Ben shrugged. "You know."

I did. A huge lump was swelling in my throat, my eyes stung and a hot anger raced through my veins. "You think you're getting picked on because your sister is Cathidy Thilver, school freak?" I spat, narrowing my eyes at him. "Newsflash: You don't need my help to be a complete loser. Let's see, you're about a foot shorter than anyone else in your class. You wear the ugliest glasses I've ever seen. And you actually think other people are interested in all your weird obsessions."

He burst into tears, shoulders shaking and his breath coming in shuddery gasps. I just stood there and hated myself. I was every bit as bad as Amber.

Finally he started walking, and I followed a couple of steps behind. We walked in silence interrupted only by the occasional sniffle from Ben. To my relief, he stopped crying before we got home. We trudged through the deep bank the snowplow had left across the foot of the driveway. The front door was locked. I set my brief-case down on the icy step and fumbled around in my pocket for the key. Mom was officially a stay-at-home mom, but lately it seemed she was doing her best to be the opposite. When Dad left for a job in the Middle East, Mom added volunteering at hospice to her usual volunteer work on the crisis line.

By five o'clock Mom still wasn't home, and I was getting hungry. I went down to the kitchen and started foraging in the cupboards. Ben was sitting at the kitchen table playing chess on his laptop. I wondered if he was still mad at me for what I'd said. "You hungry?" I asked.

He shrugged but didn't take his eyes off the screen. "What's for dinner?"

"Um, mac'n'cheese?" When it comes to cooking, I don't have a big repertoire.

"Cool."

I put a pot of water on the stove, opened the box and pulled out the little cheese packet. Then I heard the front door open and close.

Mom was home, carrying a take-out pizza in a card-board box. When Dad was here, she used to cook, but he's been away for two whole months, and he won't be back until April. In the meantime, we're eating a lot of pizza, a lot of Chinese food and a fair bit of mac'n'cheese.

"How's it going, kids?" she asked, shrugging off her coat and hanging it on the back of a kitchen chair.

I avoided her eyes. "Fine."

She nodded and sat down, running her fingers through her dark curly hair. She has great hair, and Ben does too. Me, I got Dad's straight brown hair, and light brown eyes and olive skin. Dad looks great: all tanned and outdoorsy. I just look beige all over. "Hey, Mom?" I said, putting plates on the table. "I was wondering if I could dye my hair."

She shook her head. "I don't think so. Your hair's lovely."

"It's not lovely. It's boring."

"You're twelve," she said, taking a slice of Hawaiian pizza. "You're too young to start dyeing your hair. Anyway, if you're like me you'll start going gray in your twenties, and then you'll have to dye it for the rest of your life. So don't be in a rush to start."

"I'd like it gray," I said sullenly. "I wish it would go gray now."

She sighed. "You know, Cassidy, I've spent the whole day volunteering at hospice, talking to people who are going to be dead in a few weeks or months. Could we just have a nice dinner together, minus the attitude?"

I took a slice of pizza and said nothing.

Mom smiled. "So how was your day? Anything interesting happen?"

"Well, no one died," I said. "No one was even diagnosed as terminally ill." I took a bite of lukewarm pizza. "So, no, I guess nothing interesting happened."

"If you're going to be like that, fine." She turned to Ben. "How about you, honey? How was your day?"

"Pretty good," Ben said, staring at his plate. "Um. Yeah. Nothing exceptional, but pretty good."

I guessed being bullied by Tyler and his gang couldn't compete with the soon-to-be-dead people either.

"Your dad called this morning," Mom said. "He sounds like he's doing well. Says he misses you both."

"I miss him." And I miss you too, I thought. Lately, even when she was home, she was too wrapped up in her painting to have time for us. "There's a new girl at my school," I told her. "Her name's Victoria. She just moved here."

Mom smiled hopefully. "Well, she won't know anyone then. Perhaps the two of you can be friends. Why don't you invite her over?"

"Mom! I don't even know her!"

"So, how are you going to get to know her if you don't take the first step?"

"It doesn't work like that, okay?" I hadn't brought anyone home from school in over a year. I had friends from summer camp, but they all lived too far away to see often, and I had some online friends, but as for school…well, I started getting called Cathidy at the beginning of grade six, and it had pretty much gone downhill from there.

Victoria would probably just laugh if I invited her over. I looked at my mother. "Newsflash, Mom: It's impossible to make friends unless you're exactly like all the other kids." Under the table, I tightened my hands into fists. "Impossible."

Three

The next morning, Mom was already painting by the time I got downstairs. Her studio used to be the den, but now it was completely filled with stacks of paintings leaning against walls, tables covered in paints and pastels and brushes, half-finished sketches taped up everywhere. It was chaos. She had been painting since I was a baby, but in the last couple of years she'd gotten serious about it. She had a show coming up soon, which I guess was why she was so busy. That and the dying people.

"Hi," I said.

Mom glanced up. "Is that really what you're wearing to school?"

I rolled my eyes. "Yeah, good morning to you too." I glanced down at myself: jeans, a purple scarf rolled thin and tied as a belt, and a long-sleeved black T-shirt that said *I love free speech*. I have an awesome T-shirt collection. Mom hates most of them, but she says I'm old enough to choose my own clothes.

I was about to ask what was wrong with my outfit, but when I looked up, Mom had already turned back to her painting and forgotten I was there.

In the kitchen, Ben was perched on a stool, eating a bowl of toxic-looking purple cereal and balancing a heavy book on the edge of the counter. I made some toast and peanut butter and poured a glass of milk; then I pulled another stool up to the counter and sat down beside him. He was absentmindedly stirring his cereal with his spoon while he turned pages with his other hand.

I peeked at the book he was reading. *Future Tech: Innovations in Transportation*. Typical Ben material. He might have no friends, but at least he was a genius. Presumably at some point he'd join Mensa and find other geniuses to hang out with. I, on the other hand, was just friendless. Not a genius. Not an artist. Not a brilliant engineer. Not anything special at all.

It was barely even light out when we left the house. A bank of heavy clouds hung near the horizon, and I wondered if it was going to snow again. The inside of my nose crinkled with each breath. I yanked my favorite paisley scarf up over my chin and buried my hands in my coat pockets. I'd forgotten my gloves, but I couldn't be bothered going back for them.

Ben was quiet. He was funny that way. Sometimes he'd chatter nonstop about whatever his current thing was—magnetic-levitation trains or jellyfish or the bubonic plague. And then other times, he'd go hours without saying a word. I was glad today was a quiet day. I felt bad about what I'd said yesterday, but I hadn't forgotten about what he'd said either.

We were halfway across the schoolyard when a tiny elf-like girl appeared beside us.

"Hi, Sydney," Ben said. He looked at me. "See you later."

"Aren't you going to introduce me to your friend?" I asked, curious.

He shuffled his feet a bit but finally said, "Sydney, this is Cassidy. She's, um, my sister."

Um, my sister. Like it just about killed him to admit it.

Sydney grinned at me. Pointy ears stuck out from under her blue woollen hat. "Good morning, Cassidy. A pleasure to meet you."

I nodded. Another freak. "Hi." I watched the two of them scurry off toward the school.

I couldn't believe it. Even Ben had a friend.

By the steps leading up to the school doors, Amber was showing her newly manicured nails to Madeline, Chiaki and a couple of other girls. Her nails were a hard shiny pink with tiny white daisies painted on them. She stopped talking and let her hands fall slowly to her sides when she saw me. "Oh, look. It's Cathidy. Nithe pants, Cathidy. Thalvation Army?"

I glared at her. "You got it, Amber. How about yours? Child labor in some third world country?"

"She is such a freak," Amber said to her friends, not even bothering to answer me. The other girls laughed as if Amber had said something so hysterically funny that they could barely contain themselves.

My stomach hurt. Chiaki had been my best friend, back when we were younger. We went to Brownies together in third grade. Seriously. We made friendship bracelets and played this game where you had to make thumbprints and draw faces on them and exchange them with all the other Brownies. *I'm a thumbuddy,* you had to say. Of course, with my lisp, somebody and thumbuddy sounded pretty much the same.

Anyway, I was used to Madeline and Amber being mean, but even though Chiaki had dumped me and joined the enemy halfway through grade six, I hated seeing her with them. My eyes suddenly felt hot and prickly. I pushed past the girls and ran into the school and down the hall.

Victoria was on her way out of the washroom just as I was heading in, and I practically knocked her over.

She caught my arm and pulled me back inside. "Hey, are you okay?"

I brushed tears aside with the back of my hand. "Yeth. *Yes.*"

"Was it those girls again?"

I nodded. "Always. I try not to care." I didn't know

why I was telling her all this. It wasn't something I usually talked about.

"Amber's so mean all the time. I don't get why she's popular."

"Better to be on her good side, I guess. Everyone sees how she treats the kids she doesn't like." I shrugged. "People are scared of her."

"*You* don't seem scared."

I made a face. "Newsflash: I'm a good actor."

Victoria laughed; then she sighed. "Every school I've been to has had girls like her," she said. "You know. The kind who start a stupid little club where they can decide who's in and who's out."

"They let Chiaki in," I muttered. "She used to be my friend."

She wrinkled her nose sympathetically. "You wouldn't want to hang out with them anyway."

"No, I'd just like them to leave me alone."

Victoria opened her mouth and then closed it again.

"What were you going to say?"

"We could start our own club," she said. Her eyes were bright behind her glasses and her freckled cheeks were suddenly pink.

I looked into the mirror and adjusted my hat. "Yeah, you and me and no one else."

"Maybe." She shrugged. "We'll see. Anyway, come on. We'll be late for class."

The bell rang. Crap. My heart sank. I'd seen how Mr. McMaran reacted to lateness. "Victoria…we're so dead."

She laughed. Of course, she hadn't seen McMaran—McMoron—in action yet.

He was in full rant mode about last week's math test when we entered the room. He broke off and stared at us. "So you think you can walk in here anytime you please? Whenever you feel like it? Huh? Is that what you think?"

His heavy face was several shades darker than its usual red; it was bordering on purple. His mouth was open and flecks of spit had collected at the corners. Not pretty.

I shook my head. "I apologize. Umm…" I couldn't think of an excuse. Anyway, the less I talked the better. There was a reason I'd said *I apologize* instead of *I'm sorry*: no letter *s*.

"I hate excuses. Don't give me excuses." He thwomped his hand on his desk as if he'd rather be hitting me. "And please address me as Sir."

"Ye…Okay."

Thwomp. "Now!"

I swallowed. "Thir. *Sir*." I corrected myself, but it was too late. It only drew attention to my slipup. Amber and Madeline were nudging each other, blond ponytails bobbing with delight.

McMoron smirked, enjoying my discomfort. Then he turned to Victoria and shook his big head. "The new girl. Late already. Not an auspicious beginning." He stood up and put his coffee mug on his desk. "If you can't accept responsibility for your own behavior, then there will be consequences."

I hated him. Hated him with every little cell in my body. I'd told Mom a hundred times how mean he was and she always said the same thing: *Oh, Cassidy, don't exaggerate.*

McMoron strode toward us. "The two of you can stand over here in the corner for the rest of the morning." He grabbed my shoulder with one hand and Victoria's with the other and shoved us toward the front of the room.

I turned my head to the wall. I thought I might start crying out of sheer helpless fury, but I wouldn't give Amber and Madeline the satisfaction of seeing my tears. Behind me, I could hear McMoron's footsteps returning to his desk. Then I heard a deafening crash and the sound of splintering wood.

I spun around. The teacher was sprawled on the floor, his chair broken and overturned beside him. Everyone was staring at him, wide-eyed and shocked. He struggled to his feet, his face flushed and eyes bulging. "Just tripped," he barked. "No reason for you all to stop working!"

He picked up a piece of chalk from the black-board tray, but as he stepped toward the chalkboard it slipped from his hand and shattered on the floor. He turned toward me as he bent to pick up the pieces, and I quickly turned away to face the wall again.

Then I noticed something strange: Victoria's eyes were closed. Her hands were pressed against her temples, and there was a look of intense concentration on her face.

Behind us, Mr. McMaran was swearing his head off in a way that I couldn't imagine the principal or our parents would approve of. "All right!" he bellowed. "Here is another math exercise!" Chalk squeaked against the blackboard. "You have thirty seconds. And I expect better results this time."

I waited for the sound of pencils scribbling frantically, but there was complete silence in the room. I peeked over my shoulder. Nathan's mouth was hanging open and his eyes were so wide they looked like they might pop right out. He wasn't moving. No one was moving. Then I heard a couple of smothered giggles. I turned right around to look at the class. They were all staring at the board. Mr. McMaran had written something across it, but it was sprawling, full of weird symbols and completely unreadable. I couldn't even tell if it was a math exercise at all, let alone decipher what it said.

I turned to Victoria. "Look at the board," I whispered.

She pressed her fingers harder against her temples and ignored me.

"Victoria!" I nudged her, but she didn't budge.

Something was going on. Something seriously weird.

Four

Muffled giggles were spreading across the room. Joe was chuckling out loud; Felicia was grinning like I'd never seen before; and even Nathan, who was usually scared to breathe, had his hands pressed against his mouth. Everyone was on the edge of completely losing it and only our fear of McMoron was preventing us from collapsing into helpless laughter.

All except Victoria. She had finally turned to face me, but her face was pale and tense.

Mr. McMaran pounded on his desk. *Thwomp. Thwomp.* "What is so funny? Stop that this instant!" He stepped toward the class, his face dark with anger. He grabbed his travel mug, but it leapt out of his hand and smashed to the floor. I could barely even hear the crash over the roar of laughter in the room.

"What on earth is going on in here?" Mrs. Goldstein, the principal, came running through the door, and the laughter cut off abruptly. "I could hear the noise clear down the hall. My goodness…" Her eyes flicked around the room, taking in the writing on the board, the broken chair, the travel mug. "Mr. McMaran?"

He just stood there, shaking his head. For a moment, I almost felt a little sorry for him. He looked so confused. "I'm not…I don't…" Shaking his head, he stumbled out of the classroom, slamming the door behind him.

"Well," Mrs. Goldstein said flatly. "Well." She looked around the room. "Can someone please enlighten me?"

No one said anything for a minute. Then Joe raised his hand. "I don't know, Mrs. Goldstein. Mr. McMaran kind of flipped out."

Mrs. Goldstein raised her eyebrows. "Flipped out?"

Joe just nodded. "Yeah, totally." He nodded at the chalkboard. "That's our math exercise."

She glanced at it and frowned."Is his handwriting always like that?" She studied it for a long minute, and her eyebrows flew up. "Differential calculus? For grade seven? That's…odd." She let out a long sigh. "Excuse me a moment. Please read your books, or work on whatever you were doing. I'll make arrangements." She headed out the door.

I leaned toward Victoria. "Wow."

"Mmm."

"That was bizarre. He really lost it."

She giggled. Her eyes were bright and the color was returning to her face. "Yeah."

"Are you okay? You looked sort of funny."

"I'm fine," she said quickly. "Fine." Her voice sounded funny: tight and anxious.

"You don't sound fine."

"Well, I am." She turned away from me. "Drop it, okay?"

I pulled back, feeling a bit hurt. "Sorry."

The door opened, and Mrs. Goldstein stepped back into the room. "I'll be taking the class for the remainder of the morning," she said.

By lunchtime it was snowing and windy. You might think that arctic conditions would be a reason to stay indoors, but according to Mrs. Goldstein, twenty degrees below zero wasn't cold enough for that. Everyone was whispering to each other, buzzing with questions and gossip as we funneled down the hall. *He was drunk*, I heard someone whisper. *Mrs. Goldstein was sniffing that puddle around his travel mug.*

I could believe it. Actually, it would explain a lot. But I had something else to think about, something no one else had seen: the strange look on Victoria's face while it had all been happening.

I grabbed her elbow. "Hey, come with me?"

"Okay." She shrugged on her jacket, tugged a striped wool hat over her hair and followed me outside.

The air was basically vaporized ice. "This is abusive," I muttered, trying to take shallow breaths. "The teachers all get to sit in the staff room. I swear, even my lungs are getting frostbite." There was a sheltered alcove beside the stairs, and we huddled inside it, but even out of the wind it was bitterly cold. And of course, today had to be the day I forgot my gloves.

We tucked ourselves into the corner and sat down on a piece of cardboard. It did nothing to stop the cold ground from sucking every last bit of heat out of my body. I pulled my knees up to my chest. Now that I was sitting here with Victoria, it seemed a bit silly to think she somehow had something to do with what happened in class. I didn't know why she'd had that weird look on her face, but probably she'd just had a headache or something.

It hadn't looked like a headache though. It had looked like she was concentrating. Like she was *doing* something.

"Brrrr!" Victoria said, wrapping her arms around herself. "It is soooo cold!"

"No kidding." I pushed my thoughts aside, looked at her and laughed. "Brrrrr!" I mimicked.

"What's so funny?"

"I don't know. *Brrrr.* It sounded funny. Like something my mother would say."

She laughed too. "Brrrr!"

It felt good to laugh with someone. Actually, it felt better than good. So probably I shouldn't wreck it by asking her if she'd done something in class. Something impossible.

Definitely I shouldn't. She'd think everyone was right about me. Crazy Cathidy Thilver.

But I couldn't get it out of my head.

"That was pretty wild, huh?" I ventured. "McMaran losing it like that?"

Victoria's forehead creased and she stared at the ground for a moment. "I hate bullies," she said, so softly that I had to lean toward her to hear.

"Yeah, sure. Me too." I caught my breath. "Victoria?"

Her face was closed off, warning me not to pry. But I had to know. I gave her a challenging look. "So?"

"So what?" She didn't meet my eyes.

"Victoria! Come on. You can tell me." I didn't want to say what I thought—it sounded too weird—but I was sure I was right.

"Tell you what?"

I leaned toward her. "Look, I know this sounds crazy but, well, I *saw* you! You—you made it all happen somehow."

Victoria's eyes suddenly filled with tears. She shook her head. "Cassidy, don't say anymore, okay? Please? Just forget it."

She wasn't denying it, and that was as good as admitting it, as far as I was concerned. "So you did do it! I knew it! That is so awesome. How did you do it?" I lowered my voice. "It was magic of some kind, wasn't it?"

She scrambled to her feet, brushing tears away with the back of her hand. "You don't get it! You don't understand anything. And don't say anything about it to anyone!"

"Victoria, don't be mad. I won't say anything, honest!" I reached out to her, but she was already running across the schoolyard.

Five

After lunch I headed straight back to the classroom and got there before anyone else. I was furious with myself for opening my big mouth. I slipped into my back row desk and slumped down, resting my head on my folded arms. Then I noticed that something was different. For the first time all year, the blinds had been opened, and even though the sky outside was gray, the room was filled with light.

A hand brushed my shoulder lightly. I looked up.

"Are you okay? What's your name?" The woman had curly red hair and a wide smile that showed a mouthful of braces. Since when do adults wear braces? Hers even had blue elastics which matched her shirt.

"I'm fine," I mumbled. "My name is Cassidy Silver."

"I'm Ms. Allyson. I'm subbing for Mr. McMaran." She tilted her head to one side, suddenly thoughtful. "Silver. I don't suppose you're related to Molly Silver, by any chance?"

I nodded, surprised. "Yeah. You know my mother?"

Ms. Allyson shook her head and smiled. "Only her work. But I'm a big fan. A friend of mine has one of her paintings. I could look at it for hours."

I nodded. I wouldn't say this to Ms. Allyson, or to anyone else of course, but I don't really like Mom's paintings that much. They're kind of weird: all browns and depressing dark colors with bits of glass and feathers and things stuck on them. And people say all kinds of stuff about them that I don't understand. After her last show, one critic wrote that she was a brilliant artist whose work "captured the frenetic anxiety of our times." Whatever that means. Another one said that her paintings looked like kids' summer camp projects. Dad was furious about that one, but Mom just laughed.

"Are you an artist too?" Ms. Allyson asked.

"No, not really." I hesitated. "I mean, of course I *like* art."

"Well, you should definitely be looking forward to the big art contest then."

"What art contest?"

"Mr. McMaran didn't tell you about it?" She raised her eyebrows. "Wait until everyone is here and I'll fill you in."

The other students all filed in, but there was no sign of Victoria. The desk beside me sat empty. Now that a bit of time had passed, I could think of all kinds of explanations for what had happened in the morning's class: McMaran fell off the chair and dropped the chalk because he was drunk; he wrote that weird stuff on the chalkboard because…well, maybe he used to teach high school math and he just forgot where he was. Anyway, I was sure there was an explanation that didn't involve magic. My cheeks felt hot as I remembered what I'd said: *It was magic of some kind, wasn't it?*

Jeez. Victoria must have thought I was a complete idiot. Tomorrow she'd probably be calling me Cathidy and laughing at me like everyone else. I just hoped she wouldn't repeat what I'd said.

Ms. Allyson cleared her throat. "Okay, class! I'm Ms. Allyson and I'll be teaching this class until Mr. McMaran is able to return."

A forest of hands flew up in front of me. How long would he be away? What was wrong with him? Was it true he'd been drunk? Ms. Allyson managed to answer most of them without giving us any real information beyond the official line: He was unwell and would be off work for some time. Period.

After a couple of minutes, she waved the hands down and changed the subject. "Okay, listen up. I have some exciting news for you all. There is an art contest coming up. It's open to all grade six, seven and eight students in the district. Each school will have a contest, and one winning piece of art from each school will be entered in a district-wide competition."

Joe, who rarely participated in class discussions, sat up straight. "What do you get if you win?"

The teacher smiled. "One hundred dollars plus one year's unlimited art classes at the Thomson Art Institute."

There was a flurry of excitement. Amber's hand flew up. She and Madeline were practically bouncing out of their seats. "Ms. Allyson! What kind of art do we do?"

"Anything you like," Ms. Allyson explained. "Painting, pottery, sketching, sculpture, collage. It's up to you. The theme is 'Who Are We?' So you might work on some kind of self-portrait or a work that reflects who you are in some way."

Madeline raised her hand. "Do we get to work on it in class? How long do we have?"

"The deadline for all entries is in three weeks," Ms. Allyson said. "I'll give you as much class time as I can."

Amber was looking around and smiling smugly, as if she'd already decided the prize was hers. Too bad. I wasn't going to let Amber win. No way. I imagined arriving home and telling Mom that I'd won a contest. An art contest. *Guess what?* I'd say. *I won an art contest… I'm going to be an artist.* She'd have time to listen to that, I'd bet. I imagined her face lighting up in a delighted smile, her arms stretching out toward me, her warm voice saying, *Cassidy, honey! I had no idea you were so talented.*

"Okay!" Ms. Allyson's voice shattered my little daydream. "Everyone find a partner!"

I blinked, cheeks burning. Stupid sappy fantasy. I didn't care what my mother thought anyway. I glanced around the room. Practically everyone was already paired up. Amber and Madeline were together, of course. Even Felicia already had a partner—Nathan. I stood up to look around. Was I really the only one without a partner? Newsflash: No one wants to pair up with the class freak.

I wished Victoria was here. Though, of course she probably wouldn't want to be my partner now.

"Chiaki, right? And Cassidy. It looks like you both need partners. Why don't you pair up?" Ms. Allyson ushered Chiaki into the empty desk beside mine. Victoria's desk.

I nodded at her, my teeth clenched so tight my jaw ached. My old thumbuddy. Chiaki smiled back, her face anxious beneath her dark bangs.

Ms. Allyson sat on the edge of her desk and crossed her legs. "So, before you begin thinking about your art pieces, I want you first to consider what it is about yourself that you want to convey through your art. We'll do some writing exercises, alone and with a partner, to help you get started. These exercises are to help you begin reflecting on who you are: what is important to you, how you see yourself, what challenges you face, what strengths you bring to help you meet those challenges." She broke off abruptly. "Amber, did you have a question?"

Amber was shifting impatiently in her seat. "I thought you said we had to draw a self-portrait. How come we have to do all this writing?"

Ms. Allyson nodded. "That's a good question. First, this contest isn't about drawing a picture of yourself. It's about exploring who you are."

I couldn't see Amber's face, but I'd bet she was rolling her eyes. Either that or her mouth would be hanging open.

"Writing can be a way to learn about ourselves, to uncover what lies beneath the surface that we present to the world," Ms. Allyson went on. "Try to think of writing the way an archaeologist might think of a tool she uses to uncover a treasure buried deep in the earth." Her eyes met mine for a moment.

Sitting so close to Chiaki was making me squirm, but I could have listened to Ms. Allyson all day. She wasn't like any teacher I'd ever had before.

She turned to the chalkboard and her chalk squeaked as she wrote.

If I were an animal I would be a...
Three adjectives that describe me are...
Two qualities I look for in a friend are...
One thing I am afraid of is...
I hope that someday I...

Then she turned back to the class. "Write quickly and don't think too much about your answers!"

I picked up my pen and chewed thoughtfully on the cap for a minute; then I began to write furiously. I was finishing number four when Ms. Allyson said, "Time's up!"

There was a chorus of protests and requests for more time. Ms. Allyson shook her head, her red hair flying. "No, that's it! You can discuss the exercise with your partner. You can share your answers if you wish or talk about something you learned from the exercise."

I turned to Chiaki and my stomach started knotting up. *Traitor.* "So, do you want to go first?"

She nodded, not meeting my eyes. "Okay." She looked down at her paper and smiled nervously. "Ummm. For what animal I'd be, I wrote that I'd be a cat. I really like cats."

"Huh." A mouse, more like. A scared mouse that ran around in circles, trying to impress Amber and Madeline. Maybe they were the cats. I looked down at what I'd written: *I'd be a porcupine, throwing sharp quills at anyone who got too close. Or maybe a skunk. I could spray Amber and Madeline and my old thumbuddy.* I gave her a phony smile. "I'd be a dog. A Rottweiler, maybe, or a Doberman. A dog that doesn't like cats."

The shaky smile slid off her face and her eyes widened. "Oh. Um."

"What did you put for number two?" I asked, baring my teeth. She wasn't so brave, away from her support group.

"Umm. Three adjectives that describe me? I wrote…" Her eyes met mine for a moment and suddenly she looked like she might cry. "I wrote *scared*, okay? And *stupid*. And *sorry*."

My mouth dropped open. "Are you talking about what I think you're talking about?"

She nodded and looked down at the desk.

I couldn't believe this was happening. "No one forced you to dump me," I whispered. "No one forces you to hang out with them."

"I know."

"So if you feel like that, why do you…?"

She shook her head. Her lower lip trembled and she blinked back tears. "I don't want to talk about it, okay? What did you write?"

I stared at her in disbelief. "You can't be serious. I mean, you've hardly talked to me for the last year. And that almost sounded like an apology. Almost. And now you're just changing the subject?"

She nodded. "It was an apology. It really was." She looked down at the ground and her thick bangs hid her eyes. "But…"

I finished the sentence for her. "But it doesn't change anything."

I was still Cathidy Thilver, class freak, and I wasn't going to get my thumbuddy back.

$\int_{1}^{\circ} x$

I was standing by the school's main entrance, waiting for Ben, when a flash of movement caught my eye. Victoria. She was waving at me from the other side of the cement wall that ran along the edge of the schoolyard.

"Hey!" I ran over, grinning. "I thought you were never going to speak to me again. I wouldn't have blamed you. I mean, what a lamebrain thing to say. Magic. Duh. I don't know what I was thinking…"

I broke off. Her eyes were red-rimmed and swollen. "Hey, were you crying? Are you okay?"

"I'm okay," she said. "Sorry about getting upset before. I was an idiot. Don't be mad at me, okay?"

"Me?" I let out a sigh of relief. "I'm not mad at all. Are you really okay? How come you never came back after lunch?"

"Oh, I needed to think. I had to figure out what to do." She gave a shaky sigh. "I think…well, I shouldn't tell you this, but we're friends, right?"

My heart sped up. "Tell me."

Her eyes darted from me, to the school, to the ground and back to me. She shifted from one foot to the other; then she sighed again, hesitating.

"Come on! Tell me!"

She bit her lip. "I really shouldn't. But, well, you were sort of right about what happened in class. It wasn't magic exactly, but I did have something to do with it."

"I knew it!" I yelped. "So tell me—" I broke off. Ben was racing down the steps and tearing across the schoolyard toward us, his arms and legs flying around in their usual wildly uncoordinated way. I made a face at Victoria. "That's my little brother. Hang on a sec, okay?"

Ben skidded to a halt in front of me. "Hi."

"Hey, Ben. Listen, Victoria and I need to talk privately, okay? Can you start walking home by yourself, and I'll catch up?" I saw him hesitate and added the clincher, "You know the way, right?"

It worked. "Of course I know the way," he said stiffly.

I watched him walk away. His jacket was bright red against the white snow, and he looked very small. I shook off my misgivings and turned back to Victoria.

"It's kind of a long story," she said slowly. "It's hard to know where to start."

"Mmm," I said. I didn't want to scare her off again.

"What you said before—well, it isn't exactly magic."

"Okay. Not magic," I agreed. "Stupid thing to say. Sorry about that." I tried to sound calm, but my heart was racing and my lisp tripped me up. *Thorry about that.*

Victoria didn't seem to notice. She met my eyes steadily. "Have you ever heard of telekinesis?"

It sounded familiar. "Um. I think so?"

"Telekinesis is when you can move things—like a coffee mug, say, or a piece of chalk—without touching them. By using your mind."

"That's what you did? You moved stuff, like the chalk? You made it write that weird math stuff?"

She shrugged and her eyes slid away from mine. "I guess."

"Yeah, wow." I thought for a minute. "You should've made him write something really funny. Like, I don't know, *Maths sucks.* Or *Call me McMoron.* Or…," I trailed off, trying to think what I would have picked; then I remembered what we were talking about. "Wow. Wow. This is intense. So—you're, like, psychic?"

She snorted dismissively. "I can't predict the future or read minds or anything. I just move stuff, that's all."

"Yeah, you just move stuff with your mind, that's all. That's all. Jeez, Victoria, that's, well, it's—"

"Impossible?"

I hesitated, not wanting to upset her. Then I nodded. "Yeah, kind of."

"I know." She shrugged casually. "That's what my parents said when it started happening."

My mouth dropped open. "Your parents? They know about this?"

"Of course." Victoria's voice was stronger and more confident, her chin higher. Now that she was talking about her secret—her telekinesis—she seemed more sure of herself.

"It's been happening practically my whole life," she explained. "The first time it happened I was two. I saw a toy—a stuffed elephant—on the shelf at a department store. I was pointing at it and my mom said no, we're not here to look at toys. Apparently, I threw a huge tantrum and the next thing she knew, the toy flew off the shelf and into my arms."

I shook my head. "Jeez." I was starting to feel kind of uneasy. I'd used Ouija boards at camp, but I'd never really believed in stuff like this. So it was like I didn't have anywhere in my head to put it. Every little mental compartment I tried to file it in just spat it right back out again with a big label that said *IMPOSSIBLE*. "Um, Victoria?" I said slowly. "Can you, like, show me? I mean, move something for me." I glanced around for an object and saw a discarded apple core lying on the ground. "That apple core?"

Her face crumpled. "You don't believe me."

"I do! It's just—"

"I'm not a dog," she whispered, staring at the ground. "I don't do tricks on command."

I'd blown it again. "No, look, I'm sorry. Forget I said that. I believe you, okay?"

She nodded but didn't look convinced. The confidence I'd noticed a minute ago had vanished. "My parents would kill me if they knew I told you," she said. "I'm not supposed to use telekinesis at all."

"Why not? Jeez, if I could do that stuff, I'd do it all the time." I'd have a blast, I thought. I'd move stuff around until Amber and Madeline thought they were going crazy. I'd make them leave me and Felicia and Nathan alone.

"It's not that great." Victoria frowned. "It's caused a lot of problems for me. For my family."

"What kind of problems?" I asked curiously.

Victoria gave a little shrug. "Just problems. Anyway, that's all in the past. It's all okay now."

I watched as she adjusted her glasses on her nose and tucked a stray lock of hair beneath her hat. She and I were kind of opposites, I figured. She looked ordinary but had this incredible secret. I looked—well, a bit freaky, I guess—but was secretly terribly boring. I suddenly had this incredible thought. "Victoria, you don't suppose… Could you teach me to do it? Could I learn?"

She looked taken aback. Slowly her expression turned thoughtful and then excited. "I don't know if you could learn. I've never tried to teach anyone before."

"So, maybe? You might be able to?"

She nodded. "In theory, lots of people have tele-kinetic potential, especially kids. That's what I've read anyway. And it's like anything else—if you don't practice, you can lose your ability. Like not using a muscle, you know? Probably lots of people could do it if they worked at it, but hardly anyone does." She made a face. "Most people are so narrow-minded."

"I'm not," I said quickly. "So, would you try to teach me? Please, please, please?" If she said no, I didn't think I could stand it.

"It might not work, but I don't see why we shouldn't try." She looked at me and her voice was intensely serious. "You have to swear not to breathe a word. To anyone."

"Oh, I promise! I won't say anything, not even to my brother—" I broke off abruptly. "Oh, shoot, Mom will murder me if he gets home without me. I've got to go. I'll see you tomorrow, okay?" I waved a quick good-bye; then I turned and sprinted as fast as I could, my boots slipping on the icy sidewalk.

I caught up with Ben about a block from our house. He smiled, his face lighting up. "Now we each have a friend," he said. "I have Sydney and you have Victoria."

I remembered Victoria saying that we should start our own club. Maybe we could recruit Ben and Sydney. Cathidy Thilver, school freak. Victoria Morris, telekinetic. Ben and Sydney, third grade geniuses. It was so crazy I almost had to laugh.

Seven

I had finally taken Mom's advice and invited Victoria over after school—partly motivated, I admit, by the hope that she might teach me telekinesis. Also, I wanted a demonstration. I didn't exactly think she was lying to me, but some stubborn part of my brain still couldn't quite accept it. It didn't make sense. Besides, how did Victoria know all that math stuff that she made McMoron write? Calculus, Mrs. Goldstein had said. No one in grade seven knew calculus unless they were some kind of math genius. So how could Victoria have done that?

I stood in the schoolyard, thinking and waiting for Ben and Victoria. The rush of kids funneling out the doors had slowed to a trickle. I looked at my watch, shuffled impatiently from one foot to the other and rewound my scarf around my neck more snugly.

On the other side of the fence, a skinny guy with a shaved head was pacing back and forth along the sidewalk. He kept stopping and looking up at the school.

"Hey," he called to me, "is school out already? I'm looking for someone."

I wondered who. He was maybe twenty or so, way younger than most kids' parents. Plus he looked out of place, somehow. He had a tattoo on his neck—a spider or something with tentacles. And that shaved head and really bad skin. He looked tough and a bit creepy.

I certainly wasn't going to hang around and talk to him. "Ten minutes ago," I said shortly, backing away from him. "Mostly everyone's gone except the teachers." I thought I'd mention the teachers just so he'd know there were adults around. Just in case.

He muttered something under his breath about not looking for any damn teachers and shoved his hands deep into his pockets before wandering off. I watched him go, his skinny legs weaving back and forth as he walked down the sidewalk. Maybe he was drunk. I shrugged. Whatever.

The door opened again and Victoria emerged, waving and grinning, her short brown hair tucked under her hat. "Sorry! I had to meet with Ms. Allyson about making up some work." She wrinkled her nose. "Extra math homework. Yuck."

I thought of the equations on the chalkboard again. Calculus. But it sounded as if Victoria was no math genius. I hesitated, wondering whether to ask her; then I decided not to. I didn't want to sound as though I doubted her story.

Half a block away, the creepy guy pulled away from the curb, wheels spinning in the snow. I gestured toward his car as it drove away. "Jeez, that guy sure didn't look like he was in any shape to be driving."

"What guy?"

"I don't know who he is. He was hanging around the school." I shrugged. "He seemed kind of out of it, but he said he was looking for someone."

Victoria spun around to look, but the car was gone. She stared down the empty street for a moment; then she slowly turned back to face me. "You talked to him? What did he look like?"

"He looked sort of, umm, like a drug dealer or something." I made a face. "Okay, I know that's a stupid stereotype."

She cut in, her voice urgent and her face suddenly pale. "Describe him."

I frowned. "What's the problem? You know him or something?"

There was a silence for a moment; then she laughed. "Nah. Just curious."

"Huh. You sounded kind of…," I broke off. I didn't want to pry. "Well, he was tall and skinny. Maybe twenty or so. Jeans. Shaved head. Long coat, kind of an army coat or something. And he had a tattoo of a spider or something on his neck."

Victoria didn't say anything. Her bottom lip was caught between her teeth so tightly that it was almost as white as her face.

"Are you okay? I mean, if there's something wrong,

well, you could talk to me. If you wanted too." My stomach tightened. I didn't know what was wrong, but I wished I'd never mentioned that stupid guy. I didn't get it. Victoria had just moved here. It wasn't like she'd know anyone, let alone creepy-looking guys.

She kicked at a frozen lump of snow. "Nothing to talk about," she said.

There was an awkward silence. I cleared my throat and changed the subject. "So how come you moved here anyway?" I asked.

"Um. Well, bunch of reasons, I guess." She switched her schoolbag from one shoulder to the other. "My dad got a job here. He works at a bank."

"Yeah? What does your Mom do?"

"She used to work in a veterinarian's office before we moved." She made a face. "Now she's taking some courses at the college and working part-time at a coffee shop."

"So? What's wrong with that?"

"Nothing. It's just something she and Dad are always arguing about—her being out in the evenings."

"My dad's in the Middle East." I watched the doors, waiting for Ben to appear. "He's an engineer. He gets these contracts, you know? He's been gone for months."

"Wow. Don't you worry about him? I mean…"

I shook my head. "No, it's pretty safe where he is. I miss him though." Just thinking about him made me want to cry. Mocking myself, I pretended to play a violin.

I could make a pretty good violin noise too. "The worst part is that since he left, my mom's been...I don't know." I swallowed hard and broke off. I never talked about this with anyone.

"What?"

"I don't know." I didn't know how to explain, and I kind of wished I hadn't brought it up. To my relief, Sydney and Ben meandered through the doors, chattering away to each other. "Hey, there he is." I waved. "Let's go, kid."

Ben glowered. He hated being called kid. "Sydney's coming too," he informed me, his voice cold and dignified.

I grinned at him apologetically. "I'd like to get home some time this year."

He gave me a reluctant smile, and we all set off together. It had been drizzling freezing rain all afternoon, and a thin layer of ice had formed on the surface of the snow. Our boots crunched noisily as we walked. I glanced across at the three of them, all walking almost in unison. Hmm. Obviously I wasn't really going to start a club for social outcasts, let alone hang out with a couple of third graders, but I found myself playing around with the idea anyway. What would we call ourselves, I wondered. Freaks United, maybe.

"Cassidy?" Sydney looked up at me.

"What?"

"Well, Ben and I were wondering, since there are two of us today, we don't really need you to walk us home, you know?"

I could feel my eyebrows fly up. "You guys can run ahead. I don't care."

She grinned, and the two of them shot off.

It looked as if the club was back down to two members.

Eight

Ben and Sydney were waiting on the front porch when we got home. I could hear Ben rattling on and on about the efficiency of magnetic levitation trains and his theory that the personal automobile would soon be replaced by mag-lev transportation systems. Sydney, miracle of miracles, actually looked interested. Of course, she hadn't heard it a thousand times before.

"You should've given me the key," Ben said as I stomped up the steps, kicking the snow off my boots.

"You should get your own," I retorted. "Mom's not home?"

He rolled his eyes. "She never is."

I unlocked the door, and we all tumbled in, shedding layers of hats and coats and snow-clumped boots. Sydney and Ben disappeared into the family room to play chess, and Victoria followed me up the steep stairs and into my room. She rubbed her fogged up glasses on her sweatshirt, put them back on and looked around. "Great room," she said softly.

I grinned. "Yeah, thanks. I love it."

My room was small and cozy, with a ceiling that sloped from high above the door, to very low over my tiny dormer window. A couple of years ago Mom let me pick out new paint, and we painted the walls a bright lime green. I'm kind of addicted to secondhand clothing stores and I've got some amazing clothes, way too cool to hide in a closet, so I'd covered one wall with hooks for all my scarves and hats. I love hats. Plus I have all these movie posters that I ordered online: *Rocky Horror Picture Show, Attack of the Killer Tomatoes,* stuff like that. They're fabulous. Of course, Mom won't let me watch the actual movies.

I flopped down on my bed; then I leapt up again. "Wait. We need snacks. We need vast quantities of junk food." I winked. "I want you to tell me how to do that teleky-whatsit thing, and I'm pretty sure that junk food will help me."

A minute later I was back from the kitchen, a giant-size bag of Doritos in one hand and a bag of fudge cookies in my other. "Salt or sugar? Pick your poison."

Victoria's smile was as bright as summer sunshine. "My mom always buys those puffed rice things or banana chips. Plus, we're vegetarian."

I held the chips out of her reach. "Maybe I shouldn't let you eat these. You have to build up a tolerance for this stuff gradually."

She jumped up, tried to snatch the bag from my hand and missed. "Hey! Hand them over!"

"Uh-uh. Now that I think about it, you'd better stick with your tofu burgers and steamed kelp. This stuff's full of chemicals. It might wreck your powers."

She snorted. "If you don't hand them over, I guess I'll have to use my powers to get them from you."

I wished she would, but she was obviously touchy about being asked to perform, and I wasn't going to make that mistake again. I didn't want to get my head bitten off. I handed her the chips and sat down beside her. "So, can we start? Can you show me how to move something without touching it?"

Victoria nodded. "I've been thinking about it." She looked at me, the corners of her mouth lifting in a cat-like smile. "It'd be cool if I wasn't the only one who could do this."

"I'd *love* to be the only one who could do something," I said. "Seriously. My brother is a genius, my mom is this famous artist, my dad is kind of a big shot in his field...I don't know. I'm not really good at anything."

"Sure you are," she said. "You're good at lots of things."

I nodded. "Yeah, that's the problem. I'm pretty good at lots of things. But I'm not great at anything, I can't do anything special. I sure can't do something that no one else can do."

"Yeah, well, believe me, it's not so wonderful." Victoria didn't meet my eyes, and again I had the feeling there was something she wasn't telling me. I was debating whether to ask her about it when she snapped her eyes back to mine and flashed me her big pink-gums-and-little-white-teeth smile.

"Okay," she said. "I think the best way to start is to do an exercise to help you feel the energy that you need if you want to move an object." She sat up, crossed her legs and faced me. "Okay. Hold your hands like this."

I copied her, holding my hands so that my palms faced each other. Her fingers were curved and her fingertips not quite touching.

"Now close your eyes and imagine that there is a green energy surrounding you—close your eyes! Okay, now focus on that energy and try to move it into the middle of your hands."

I opened one eye. "Move it? Umm, how exactly do I move imaginary energy?"

Victoria frowned. "Try to visualize it. Picture it. It's real, you just can't see it. Once you learn more, you will be able to feel it. At least I hope so. Trust me, okay?"

I closed my eyes again. "Okay...I'm visualizing the energy." Lime green or forest green, I wondered. I tried not to giggle. It was like being at camp with those girls who brought the Ouija board: everyone else all solemn, and me sitting there with my fingers on the sliding plastic thing, thinking how crazy it all was. Except, I reminded myself, this time it wasn't. This time it was for real.

"Okay. Now imagine that the energy is moving into the space between your hands. Keep taking slow deep breaths. Imagine the energy getting denser and denser, forming a ball of energy between your hands."

Nothing happened. After a few minutes, I broke the silence. "What's supposed to happen?"

"You didn't feel anything at all?"

"No, not really."

"Don't get discouraged, okay? Maybe it'll take practice." She smiled, but I couldn't help wondering if she was disappointed in me.

"What should have happened?"

"You should feel some pressure between your hands. You know if you put two magnets together the wrong way? And they push each other away? It feels kind of like that."

"Maybe if you showed me?" I asked hopefully.

She bit her lip and frowned. "I told you. I'm not allowed."

I sighed. "Okay. Sorry. I'll try again." I put my hands together and closed my eyes. There was a knock at the door, and my eyes flew open. "What?"

Ben opened the door and poked his head in. "Dinner's ready."

"No! Seriously? Don't tell me you made something."

He shook his head. "No, Mom's home. She brought Chinese."

Mom was unpacking cartons and putting plates on the table.

"Sorry," she said as we came in. "I know I said I'd cook tonight, but I got held up. Got a really serious call on the crisis line and couldn't get away."

"You got your hair done," I said accusingly. She didn't look like herself at all. Her dark curls were gone and instead she had a sleek chin-length bob.

Her hand flew to her hair. "This morning. What do you think?"

"It's gorgeous," Victoria said shyly. "You look like an actress or something."

Mom laughed, shaking her head so that her hair swung smoothly from side to side. "Thank you. You must be Victoria."

I opened the fridge and grabbed a jug of filtered water and a big bottle of soda. "What do you want to drink?"

"Oh." Victoria turned to look at me and picked a glass up from the table. "Water's fine."

Ben and Sydney came running in. They reminded me of a couple of little wind-up toys, always buzzing from one place to another.

Ben sat down and Sydney dropped into the chair beside him. "Wow," he said. "We look like a big family.

Imagine if Victoria and Sydney were our sisters and there were always five of us here."

"Six," I said quickly. "Don't forget Dad."

"Six, then," Ben agreed. "Hey, Victoria? Do you have any siblings?"

I laughed. Siblings. Ben's vocabulary cracked me up.

There was a pause, and I turned to look at Victoria. The glass slipped from her hand and smashed on the floor. Broken glass all over. "Oh," she gasped, "I'm so sorry."

"Oh, don't worry," Mom said quickly. "They're nothing special, just cheap ones." She bent to get the brush and dustpan from under the sink.

"Let me do that," Victoria said, reaching for the brush.

Mom hesitated before she handed it to her. "Be careful," she said. "Don't cut yourself."

Ben had forgotten the conversation and was chatting with Sydney about their chess strategies. I watched Victoria sweep. Her face was pale and her hand was shaking slightly. I hadn't forgotten what Ben had asked her.

And I was ninety-nine percent sure she hadn't dropped that glass by accident.

Nine

The next day, Ms. Allyson was back. I hoped Mr. McMaran would be away for a long, long time like until the end of the school year. Not because I didn't want to see him again, though obviously I didn't, but because I really liked Ms. Allyson. It was the first time in ages that I'd actually been interested in anything we were doing in the classroom.

Our first class was Social Studies. I had hoped to pair up with Victoria, but Ms. Allyson had us number off to form groups. We were going to be having a class debate on whether or not it was better to be alive today than at any other time in human history. It didn't matter what you really thought. I was in group four, and therefore I had to argue that it was.

I grabbed a pen and my notebook and walked across the classroom to join the other number fours in the front corner. Nathan and Felicia had pulled a couple of desks together and were already sitting down, their expressions apprehensive. Amber was pulling up a chair to join them. A look of dismay crossed her face when she saw who she was stuck with, and my stomach clenched tight. No doubt she'd be less than thrilled to discover she was stuck with me too. I looked around for Victoria. She was a number two, along with Madeline, Chiaki, Joe and a couple of others. I caught her eye and felt a little better. I winked at her; then I took a deep breath and dragged myself over to my group.

Amber took one look at me and groaned. "What *is* this? Ms. Allyson must hate me."

"Yeah, sucks to be you," I said, meeting her eyes. I didn't want her to know how nervous she made me. I lifted my chin a little higher. What could she really do to me anyway? So what if she thought I was a loser. If I had to choose between having no friends or hanging out with Amber, I'd pick no friends. A smile twitched at the corners of my lips as I remembered. I had a friend. I had Victoria. And I was going to be telekinetic. Beat that, Amber.

"What are you smiling about?" Amber spat.

The butterflies in my stomach felt more like small birds, crashing around wildly. I ignored them and grinned widely, just to annoy her.

Felicia cleared her throat. "Umm, shall we start by brainstorming ideas? I can take notes if you want."

Amber was quick to pounce. "Who died and appointed you group leader?"

"Sorry," Felicia muttered, looking down at the desk. There was a long silence. Nathan looked like he was trying to be invisible. Felicia had picked up her pen and started doodling on the margins of her paper. Amber was staring at me.

"What?"

Amber smiled at me. Not her usual smirk but something that resembled an actual smile. "Can you believe her nerve? She's like the last person we'd want as group leader. I mean, I can't even understand her, her accent is so weird."

This was freaking me out. Amber being mean I could handle, but Amber smiling at me was scary. It slowly dawned on me that she was looking to me for support. Apparently she had decided that while Cathidy Thilver might be a bit of a freak, Felicia was even more of a loser.

Too bad for Amber. I took a deep breath to steady my voice. "I don't know what you're talking about."

Amber's mouth fell open slightly. Inside my stomach, the birds turned back into butterflies and folded up their wings. "Felicia sounds fine to me," I said. "I think her accent is cool." I turned to Felicia and grinned. "You're from New Zealand, right?"

Felicia nodded gratefully and pushed her heavy dark hair off her face. "I am. I lived in Auckland. We moved to Canada two years ago. I still have lots of family back there."

I'd never heard her say so much all at once.

There was a moment's silence, and then Nathan broke in shyly, "I like her accent too. And I think she'd be a good group leader." He grinned at me and Felicia, his skinny face lighting up.

An odd expression flickered across Amber's face. Disconcerted. If I didn't know better, I'd say she looked afraid. For once, she was at a loss for words.

I cleared my throat and turned to the others. "So shall we brainstorm then? Like Felicia suggested?" I chewed on the end of my pen and tried to think about the assignment. "It seems to me that whether this is a good time to live in totally depends on who you are. Like, if you're a kid in Afghanistan or Iraq, now is not so good. But if you're black and live in the States, now is probably better than a hundred years ago."

"Mmm. But still not so good," Nathan pointed out. "And Canada isn't that different."

I looked at him in surprise. I'd never heard him voice an opinion before. "True enough," I acknowledged.

Felicia tapped her pen on the table. "We're not supposed to debate it," she pointed out. "We just have to argue that now is better."

Amber hadn't said a word. I snuck a sideways peek at her. "What do you think, Amber?"

She shrugged uncertainly. "I guess now is okay."

"Riigght," I drawled. "Words of wisdom from Amber, who thinks now is okay."

Amber flushed and turned her face away. I felt a heady surge of power, an odd exhilaration. Then I looked at Amber again and a wave of shame swept over me. I bit my lip. "Umm, Amber? I didn't mean that. I'm thorry. *Sorry.*"

She looked right at me and gave me a tiny almost-smile. "It's okay. It's okay, Cassidy."

Cassidy. Not Cathidy. Cassidy.

That afternoon, Ms. Allyson had blocked off some time for us to work on our art projects. The contest deadline was only two weeks away, and I hadn't even started. Actually, that's not quite true: all I had done was start. Over and over. Start one thing, mess it up, toss it out, start another. I couldn't seem to figure out what I wanted to do.

Who Are We? I sighed. What the heck did that mean? I pulled out my notes and read over what Ms. Allyson had said. *Writing can be a way to learn about ourselves, to uncover what lies beneath the surface…like a tool an archeologist uses to uncover a treasure buried deep in the earth.* Well, I wasn't convinced there were any treasures to unearth, but maybe writing would at least be something to do. I couldn't face too many more crumpled up paintings and squashed clay sculptures.

I picked up my pen and flipped to a new section of my notebook. In bold letters, I wrote: *Who is Cassidy Silver?*

Ms. Allyson walked behind me and paused for a moment. "That," she said in a low voice, "is a very good place to start." She rested her hand briefly on my shoulder, and suddenly I missed my mom more than ever. Maybe tonight I'd try to talk to her. Maybe. I chewed on my pen for a moment; then I started to write.

Cassidy Silver misses her mom. Cassidy Silver wonders how you talk to someone who doesn't have time to listen. I thought about that for a moment. It wasn't quite fair. *Okay, sometimes she has time to listen, but how can I complain about my trivial little problems when she spends all day talking to people who have cancer or are suicidal or drug addicted or whatever? I always imagine she must be wondering how her kid ended up so self-centered and petty.* I broke off. This wasn't really about who I was. Or was it?

Unlike her brilliant family, I wrote, *Cassidy Silver has no amazing talents.* I stared at the words for a moment and a slow smile spread across my face. I was going to learn telekinesis, and you couldn't get much more amazing than that.

Ten

Ever since I'd had Victoria over to my place, she'd been saying she should invite me over to hers. A few days later, she finally did.

"Mom and Dad want to meet you," she said. She looked uncomfortable. "So, if you want to come over, you can. But you don't have to. We could go to your place."

I was dying to go: I'd been practicing telekinesis every day, and I still hadn't had any success. Maybe another lesson would help. Still, it sounded like she was only inviting me because her parents told her to. "Do you want me to come?" I asked.

"Yeah, I guess."

I frowned. "Gosh, do you think you could sound a little less enthusiastic?"

We were sitting at our desks in the back row, waiting for class to start. Victoria lowered her voice and leaned closer. "Sorry. I want to see you after school. It's just… well, it's kind of complicated. My parents don't get along that well and they're not a heap of fun to be around. Plus, they'll ask you too many questions. They always do that."

"It'll be just the four of us then?" I asked, remembering how she'd avoided Ben's question about siblings.

She nodded, looking surprised. "Of course. Who else would be there?"

"I don't know. Just wondering. Anyway, I would like to come, and don't worry about your parents." I made a face. "At least they're both there."

Victoria lived farther from school than I did, and in the opposite direction—toward town rather than away from it. After school we cut through the yard toward the bus stop, pulling our hats down firmly over our ears as the cold wind whipped tiny flecks of icy snow against our faces. Ben had already left with Sydney. Apparently Sydney had been given a science kit for Christmas, and she and Ben were going to spend the rest of the day extracting DNA from a kiwi fruit.

"So, you think we could work on the telekinesis thing again?" I asked.

"Course we can."

"Cool. I was thinking, maybe if I—" I stopped dead. "Hey, there's that guy again. See, by the bus stop?" I pointed. "He's the one I told you about, remember? The guy who was here the other day?"

Victoria grabbed my arm and pulled me behind a nearby Dumpster. "Shhh," she whispered urgently.

I remembered how strangely Victoria had reacted when I mentioned him before. "What is it? Do you know him?"

"I don't want him to see me, okay? So, let's just wait here. Maybe he'll leave."

I squatted behind the Dumpster and watched the man. He was talking with the kids who were waiting for their bus. Beside me, Victoria was so still I thought she must be holding her breath.

"What's wrong?" I whispered. "Who is he?"

She shook her head and motioned to me to be quiet.

I remembered Ben's question again, and how Victoria had dropped the glass to avoid answering it. I bent even closer so that my mouth was right next to her ear. "Is he your brother?"

Her eyes widened in surprise. Then she nodded silently. The school bus pulled into view, driving slowly on the icy road. I started to get up, but Victoria grabbed me and pulled me back down.

"Come on," I whispered. "We'll miss the bus."

She looked all wobbly, like she might start to cry. "We'll have to walk. I can't let him see me."

I studied the guy. Her brother. It seemed so unlikely. He must be at least ten years older and he sure didn't look like the kind of guy I'd want for a big brother. Obviously not the kind Victoria wanted either, judging by her reaction.

The kids all trooped single file onto the bus, and the bus slowly pulled away, its wheels spinning slightly in the snow. Victoria's brother headed down the sidewalk, away from the school. He had gone about half a block and was starting to disappear in the blowing snow when he ducked into a small red car parked by the curb. Then, skidding slightly, the car pulled out and disappeared around the corner.

I turned to Victoria. Her face crumpled and she started crying: shoulder-shaking, breath-gasping sobs. I put my arm around her a bit awkwardly and gave her shoulders a squeeze. "Do you want to tell me what's going on? How come you don't want him to see you?"

"Let's wait here for a moment to be sure he's gone, okay?" She managed to stop crying, gulped a bit and rubbed her eyes with her gray mittens. "Then I guess we're going to have to walk home. It's kind of a long way."

"Okay, fine. We'll walk. I don't care, as long as you fill me in."

Victoria sighed. "His name's Rick. He's my dad's son from his first marriage—my half-brother."

"He's a lot older than you."

"Ten years. He's twenty-two." She stood. "Let's start walking. I'm freezing."

I straightened up gratefully and stomped my feet against the hard ground, trying to get the feeling back into my toes.

Victoria kept talking, fast, as if she'd been bottling it all up for a long time. "Rick's always had problems. By the time I started grade one, he'd dropped out of high school. He started getting in trouble, breaking into houses and stealing cars. Mom and Dad used to fight about it all the time."

"So he lived with you?"

"Just weekends and holidays with us. He and my mom never got along." She glanced sideways at me. "Dad blames himself. He thinks the divorce is why Rick's so messed up."

Lots of kids have divorced parents, I thought. Mostly they didn't steal cars or break into houses. "What do you think?" I asked, keeping my voice neutral.

She pushed her hat down more firmly on her head and was quiet for a moment. "I don't know why Rick does the stuff he does." She shrugged. "He probably doesn't even know."

"So why don't you want to see him?"

She wiped her eyes with the back of her mitten, shoved her hands deeper into her pockets and stared at the ground. "He knows about me being telekinetic," she said, her voice low. "Back when I was a kid, he used to get me to do stuff for him. He'd make it like a game."

A shiver ran down my back. "What kind of stuff?"

"Pretty harmless stuff at first. You know, playing jokes on people. Like he'd get me to make someone's hat fall off over and over, or make their fly come unzipped.

Rick would laugh his head off, and I guess I liked the attention." She shrugged. "I was maybe five or six when it started, I don't remember."

"That doesn't sound so bad." Actually it sounded pretty funny. I thought of Amber and wished Victoria would still do tricks like that.

"No, but then we started doing other things. He'd point out the wallet in someone's back pocket and tell me to slide it out real slowly, so the guy wouldn't even notice. I'd let it drop to the ground. We'd wait until the guy walked around the corner, and then Rick would pick it up."

"Stealing," I said flatly. "He used you to steal?"

She nodded. "I didn't even know it was wrong when we started, but by the time I was in third grade, we were stealing all kinds of stuff. Cameras, iPods, those charity cash boxes at grocery stores, women's purses." She looked sideways at me. "I knew it was wrong by then."

"But you kept doing it?"

"I guess you probably think that's awful."

I hesitated. "Couldn't you have told your mom?"

There was a long pause. "My mom isn't always that easy to talk to," she said at last. "And I didn't want to get in trouble, you know? Like I said, I knew it was wrong."

I didn't say anything.

"I looked up to him, you know? He made everything fun." Victoria's mouth tightened. "Then we got caught," she whispered. "I was eight. Rick was almost eighteen.

He got charged with theft. My parents had a big fight. I could hear them from my room. And the next day they told Rick he couldn't stay with us anymore."

"Good."

"Yeah, for a while it was good. We didn't see much of him for a couple of years." She bit her bottom lip and stared down at the ground. "I've never told anyone before."

"I'm glad you told me," I said. "I'm glad you trust me." I meant it, but as soon as I said the words I felt a tiny niggling doubt. She trusted me, but I didn't quite trust her. I couldn't shake this feeling there was something she wasn't telling me. And I still wasn't sure I believed in telekinesis.

Eleven

Victoria's house was bigger and newer than mine: a square box with a double garage and a big evergreen tree on the front lawn. She let us into a glossy front hall—all glass-paneled doors and marble floors—and I tried not to stare. I untied my boots, slipped them off and lined them up neatly with the rows of shoes on the mat.

"We're still unpacking," Victoria said apologetically, gesturing to the empty bookshelf in the huge living room and the piles of boxes lining one wall. "Come up to my room. It's cozier."

I nodded. The living room wasn't exactly inviting.

Victoria's bedroom was at the end of the upstairs hallway. She opened the door and stood back to let me go in first. I stepped inside and looked around.

"What do you think?"

The room was certainly smaller, but I wouldn't have called it cozy. A neatly made-up bed, a dresser with a hairbrush lying on it, bare white walls. It had the same not-quite-lived-in look as the living room. I tried to keep my expression the same. "It's nice," I said. "I guess maybe you haven't quite finished yet?"

Victoria glanced around the room and shrugged. "We've moved three times in four years. It doesn't seem worth going to a lot of trouble fixing up my room if we're only going to leave anyway."

A new worry twisted in my stomach like a cold fist. "You won't move again, will you? You won't leave?"

Victoria's eyes were bloodshot and her nose was pink from crying. She tucked her hair behind her ears and said nothing.

"You can't move," I said. "I don't want to go back to having no one to hang out with."

"You'd have people to hang out with," she said.

I snorted. "Like who?"

"Joe, for one."

"Joe! What are you talking about?"

She giggled. "He likes you."

My cheeks were on fire. "He does not!"

"When we had to do that debate thing, remember? The one about whether it's better to live now—"

"Yeah, yeah, I remember. So what?"

She giggled again. "Joe was in my group, and he asked me about you. Well, he asked if I knew where you got that T-shirt you were wearing."

I sighed with relief. "That doesn't mean he likes me."

"Sure it does."

"Victoria! Cut it out. It does not." I remembered what we'd been talking about before she decided to totally embarrass me. "Anyway, I don't want you to move."

"And I don't want to move. I hate moving. But we always end up moving." She took her glasses off and turned them around in her hands. Without them, her eyes looked bigger and bluer.

"Why? How come you move so much?"

"I don't know. My parents always think that everything is better somewhere else. And when Rick starts hanging around, things always get messed up." Victoria rubbed her hands across her eyes; then she put her glasses back on. "Usually Dad lends Rick money, and Mom gets mad. Last time we moved was because Dad kept missing work, trying to bail Rick out of some problem, so he got fired."

"Do you think they know Rick's in town?"

She groaned. "I don't know. I don't even want to think about it. They're not fighting so much right now, but if he starts hanging around, they'll start fighting again. They always do."

"Yeah, wow." I stared at her, trying to imagine what that would be like. My parents drive me crazy sometimes but they don't fight, ever. Or at least if they do, they never do it when Ben and I are around. "Are you going to tell them Rick's here?" I asked.

"I guess I have to," Victoria said hesitantly. "Mom thinks he's dangerous. Don't you think I should tell them?"

I shrugged, trying to look like I thought it was no big deal either way. "Sounds like it just causes problems."

"I couldn't stand it if everything got all messed up and we ended up moving again," she whispered. "I know he's my brother and I guess this sounds awful, but I just want him to stay out of our lives. And I hate changing schools." She looked up at me. "Especially now that I've found somebody to be my best friend."

Somebody, thumbuddy. I felt a twang of guilt: What if Rick really was dangerous? I was being about as good a friend to Victoria as Chiaki had been to me. I opened my mouth to say that maybe she should tell her mom after all, but before I could speak, Victoria shook her head. "No, I won't tell them. It's better not to say anything." She looked at me with a forced smile. "So, now what?"

There was a weird, hot, gnawing feeling in my belly. I ignored it and changed the subject. "Are you going to teach me how to start moving things or what?"

First, Victoria made me do the exercise she had taught me before. I wasn't too hopeful about it working. As I sat on Victoria's bed and placed my hands together to begin gathering energy, I calculated that I'd probably practiced this exercise at least a hundred times since she'd showed it to me. Once or twice I'd thought that I might have felt something happening: a sensation of warmth between my hands, a subtle pressure. Way too subtle.

"Okay," said Victoria. "Can you feel the ball of energy between your hands?"

"Umm, I think so? Maybe?"

"Okay, now focus on that energy and bring your hands to your chest. Imagine that energy flowing into your body."

I felt a rush of warmth in my hands and opened my eyes, startled. "I felt it! Wow. Oh, wow, I think maybe I really felt something."

Victoria was smiling and nodding at me like crazy. "That's great. That's a good sign." She placed her school binder, closed, on the bed in front of my crossed legs. On top of it, she laid a small white feather. "We're going to start with something light. I want you to focus all of that energy on this feather. Imagine the energy flowing toward it. The energy is like an extension of you: you can direct it and use it like you would use your own hands… Keep breathing."

I let out my breath. I hadn't realized I was holding it. Nothing was happening to the feather. I squinted at it. Maybe if I blew on it ever so slightly…I just wanted to see the stupid thing move. I sighed and tried to focus on the energy.

After a few minutes, Victoria interrupted me. "That's enough, Cassidy. It's going to take time and practice, I guess."

"Can't I try something else?"

"You'll give yourself a headache. Anyway, I just heard

Mom come in." She frowned. "Don't tell her about this, okay? She'd flip out."

"Sure, no problem."

"Seriously," she said. "Promise me."

I nodded, surprised. "Okay. I promise." A thought popped into my head—a nasty, disloyal thought—and I tried to push it away quickly. But it was too late. The thought wouldn't leave, and I could tell already it was going to hang around and pollute everything with doubt and distrust and endless questions. What if Victoria wasn't telekinetic at all? What if the real reason she didn't want me to say anything was because her parents would laugh and wonder what I was talking about? What if this entire thing—Rick, the telekinesis, all of it—was just a big dramatic story?

Twelve

Victoria's dad walked in the front door just as we arrived at the bottom of the stairs. He raised his eyebrows at me. "Hello. You must be Cassidy."

"Hi," I said, feeling suddenly shy. Shyness isn't a problem I usually have, but for some reason I was nervous about meeting Victoria's parents.

"We've heard lots about you," he said.

I nodded and looked away. I don't know why people say that. It always makes me uncomfortable, knowing that people have been talking about me.

Victoria's mom appeared in the doorway. "Oh, perfect timing. Dinner's just out of the oven." She nodded at me as she ushered us all into the dining room. "Hello, Cassidy. Good to meet you."

At my house, we usually ate in the kitchen. Even when Dad was home and we had proper dinners instead of take-out, we just sat around the kitchen table. And we didn't set the table, exactly. I mean, obviously we used plates and forks and all that, but we usually got our own utensils or else someone plunked a pile of cutlery and maybe a roll of paper towels on the table.

Victoria's house couldn't have been more different. The table was set with salad bowls and plates and cloth napkins, not to mention a bewildering variety of forks and spoons at each place. I sat down and hoped I wouldn't embarrass myself too badly.

Victoria's mother dished the salad and filled our glasses with water. Then she turned to me. "So, Cassidy," she said, "tell us a bit about yourself."

I squirmed. "Not much to tell," I said. I glanced around the room, hoping for inspiration, and my gaze fell on a pair of portrait-style photographs sitting on the sideboard. One was a toddler, a little girl with brown hair and a slightly anxious gummy smile. Victoria. The other was a boy around our age, with freckles and a wide grin. Rick, maybe?

"Uh, so how do you like it here?" I asked.

"Well, it seems very nice. I've been pretty busy. I'm taking some classes at the college." She smiled at me. "Computers, you know? I need to bring my skills up to date. It all changes so fast."

I nodded. Grownups always complained about that. "Who are the pictures of?" I asked, nodding toward the photographs.

Victoria looked at me; then she looked down at her plate.

Her dad shoveled a forkful of lettuce into his mouth and chewed silently. Her mom smiled again, but a little stiffly. "That's Victoria, back when she was two. Cute, huh? And the other picture, the boy, that's my stepson, Rick."

I couldn't tell if there really was a sudden chill or if it was just my imagination.

"Well," Victoria's mom said brightly, "I hope you like tofu and spinach casserole? It's one of Victoria's favorite meals." She dished a pile of steaming green slop onto my plate. "Victoria tells me that your mother is an artist. That's very interesting."

I nodded. People always said it was interesting when they totally couldn't relate.

"I was thinking about taking an art class," she mused.

Victoria's dad raised his eyebrows. "And when exactly would you fit that in?"

She shrugged. "Maybe if you actually cooked a meal or helped clean up the house occasionally, I'd have time to do something that actually interested me."

He didn't respond. We all ate in silence for a few minutes. I stared down at my plate. I wasn't crazy about vegetables, especially green ones. The food felt like grass in my mouth. Hot chewy grass. I forced down a few mouthfuls.

After a while, Victoria's parents started talking to each other in strained polite voices about her dad's day at work, and whether the car needed an oil change, and how much longer winter was going to drag on for. Victoria and I kept catching each other's eyes, and for some weird reason I had an awful urge to start giggling. It was a relief when dinner was over and we could finally retreat to her room.

Victoria wanted me to keep practicing telekinesis, but I couldn't forget my earlier doubts. All those questions were still tumbling around in my head like clothes in a dryer. I kept staring at the feather and wondering if this whole thing was real or not. I wanted it to be real more than anything. It was my one chance to escape being so ordinary.

After several more attempts, the little white feather still lay stubborn and unmoving. I couldn't concentrate. I hadn't felt that surge of energy again either. I gave an exaggerated groan. "I am never going to get this! Isn't there something else I can try?"

Victoria shrugged. "I don't know. I've never tried to teach anyone this stuff before. And I never had to learn it. It just happened."

"I really thought I felt something, before dinner," I said. "I guess I just imagined it."

"Maybe you should go back to practicing that exercise. You know, see if you can get that feeling again and then try to capture that energy."

"Mmmm." I stared at the feather, blinking back tears.

She looked at me helplessly. "I'm sorry. I know you really want to do this. Maybe it's not something that can be taught."

We sat in silence for a few minutes. Downstairs, I could hear Victoria's parents cleaning up the kitchen and washing the dishes. I thought of my own chaotic house. I'd rather have that chaos—the take-out pizzas, my mom distracted and busy, my dad off in the Middle East—than the tension and silence in Victoria's show-home.

"Don't give up," Victoria said suddenly. "Please don't give up. I've never known anyone else who could do this stuff, you know? I'd love to not be the only one."

"Yeah, well, I'll keep trying." I studied her face and wondered if I was making a complete fool of myself. I still had absolutely no idea if she was lying to me.

Thirteen

Back when we had Mr. McMaran, English classes had been deadly boring. All we ever did was take turns reading aloud from the textbook. It was different with Ms. Allyson. She never said so, but I was pretty sure she didn't think much of textbooks. We had just skimmed three chapters in five minutes and now she wanted us to do something she described as warm-up exercises. I had visions of the whole class doing jumping jacks and wondered what exactly she had in mind.

"All right," said Ms. Allyson, "get into groups of three. Quick, quick!" She was perched on a stool, swinging one foot back and forth, wearing red leather cowboy boots which almost matched her hair.

Ms. Allyson sure liked to make us work in groups. I glanced across the aisle at Victoria, who quickly scooted her chair over to join me. We needed a third. For some stupid reason, I found myself looking over to where Chiaki sat. She had already joined Amber and Madeline.

Maybe Joe? Then Felicia turned around to look at us. She hesitated; then she got up and walked back to where we sat.

"Do you think I could work with you two?" she asked in a low voice.

I hesitated for a second. Hanging out with Felicia was only going to make Amber despise me more. Then I felt a flush of shame for even thinking that way. I pushed the thought aside and smiled at Felicia. "Sure," I said. Then I laughed. "All those tormented by the Amber-Madeline alliance are welcome here. We're going to form our own alliance and take over."

Felicia looked slightly alarmed. "Take over?"

"She's just kidding around," Victoria told her. She gave me a stern look. "Don't scare off the new recruits."

"Recruits?" Felicia's voice rose an octave.

I laughed. "Sorry. It's just that we've been talking about how annoying it is, the way Amber and Madeline give certain people—like me—a hard time."

"And me." Felicia's forehead was still creased, but a smile was playing at the corners of her mouth.

"Especially you," I conceded. "You are probably number one on their list of people to be nasty to."

She gave me a long look. "Not so much, since you and Nathan stood up for me that day. You know, the debate thing?"

"Really? Huh." I was surprised. I'd figured sticking up for Felicia might annoy Amber, but I hadn't really expected it to make her back off. I hadn't expected it to make Felicia want to hang out with me either.

"Power in numbers," Victoria said. "We outsiders have to stick together."

Ms. Allyson cleared her throat behind us. "Um, have you three finished plotting?"

I blushed. Plotting? Had she been listening to us?

"Here's the first exercise," she said. She smiled and handed me a small piece of paper.

I read it out loud. "You are going to write a short poem together. On one piece of paper, you will each write one word in turn. Go fast and don't criticize each other's words. Nonsense is fine. Just keep passing the paper around and take turns adding a word."

Felicia giggled. "This is cool."

It sounded kind of silly, but I was okay with that. "You start," I said.

Felicia bent over our paper, giggling. "Outside," she said, writing fast.

I took the paper from her and tried to think of a good word.

"Write fast," Victoria reminded me.

I shrugged. "Is."

"Not," said Victoria. She slid the paper back to Felicia.

Felicia laughed. "Is? Not? Come on guys, don't make me do all the work." She chewed on her thumbnail for a moment. "So bad."

"Hey, I thought you were only allowed one word," I said.

"You are," Victoria said. "But leave it. I like it."

I laughed. "You're such rebels."

"Uh-huh," Felicia said. "Your turn. One word for you."

By the time Ms. Allyson told us to stop writing, all three of us were laughing hysterically.

"Shall we read them out loud?" she suggested.

Victoria shook her head at me frantically. "We can't," she whispered.

I looked at Felicia and raised my eyebrows. "Well?"

"Do it," she said.

I turned to Victoria. "Let's do it. Why not?"

She bit her lip. "Okay. Do it."

Ms. Allyson looked around the room. "Any volunteers to go first?"

Amber was bouncing off her seat, waving one hand in the air.

"Amber?"

"Okay." She cleared her throat. "A turtle ate my breakfast and followed me to school. The teacher said, that's against the rule. So the turtle jumped into a swimming pool."

Ms. Allyson laughed. "Great. It's fun, isn't it? Who's next?"

I raised my hand.

"Cassidy. Go ahead."

I dropped my eyes to the paper and read aloud.

"Outside is not so bad. Things can be seen more clearly from the outside. On the outside, there is more room to move around."

There was a hush in the classroom for a moment. I looked around. Chiaki turned to look at me; then she quickly ducked her head so I couldn't see her expression.

"Nice work," Ms. Allyson said finally. "Very nice."

I sat down, blushing. We'd just been kidding around, but reading our poem out loud had actually given me goose bumps. I meant every word of it. I hadn't realized it before, at least not so clearly: I didn't mind being on the outside. I just wanted some other outsiders to be there with me.

After school, Victoria and I talked in the schoolyard while I waited for Ben. A light snow was falling. I lifted my face and stuck out my tongue to catch a snowflake. The sun shone in my eyes, and I felt like laughing out loud for no reason at all.

"I'm so glad Felicia joined our group today," Victoria said.

I nodded thoughtfully. I could put on a good show of not caring what others thought, but Victoria, in her quiet way, didn't seem to care at all. I grinned at her. "Me too. I don't give a hoot what Amber Patterson thinks." I raised one eyebrow. "Speak of the devil. Look who's coming our way."

Amber, Madeline and Chiaki were sauntering arm in arm. As usual, Amber spoke for them all. "So, you two are hanging out with Fat Felicia now, huh? That's pretty sad."

I narrowed my eyes. "No, Amber. What's sad is the way you cling to this stupid idea that you are better than anyone else."

"So who died and appointed you god?" Amber snapped.

"No one died. I've always held that position. And it's goddess, if you don't mind."

Victoria giggled.

"You two are so weird. And Cassidy, that hat is the ugliest thing I've ever seen." She made a face. "Yuck, here comes your fat little friend." She pointed at Felicia, walking down the school steps toward us. "Come on, Madeline, Chiaki—let's go. I smell something bad coming this way." She wrinkled her nose, grabbed her friends' arms and marched off.

I scowled, wishing I'd been able to think of something sharp and funny to say—I hated to let her have the last word. I was staring after them when Chiaki suddenly twisted around and mouthed a silent "Sorry" over her shoulder.

Amber yanked on her arm. "Come on, Chiaki. I said, let's go."

My old thumbuddy. I wondered why she let Amber boss her around and remembered her turning to look at me when I read our poem. Maybe the outside was starting to look good to her.

"I like your hat," Victoria said.

"Mmm. Me too." It was one of my favorites: a floppy black one woven with sparkly threads. I adjusted it on my head and grinned at Felicia, who was approaching us shyly. "Hi," I said. "You just missed a friendly visit from the Demonic Duo and their sad sidekick."

"Chiaki?"

"Yeah." I shrugged, wishing I felt as unconcerned as I sounded.

"You guys used to be friends?" Felicia asked.

I didn't want to talk about it. "Uh-huh. I guess she decided she could do better."

There was an awkward moment of silence. Then Victoria grinned at me. "She was wrong."

I nodded, gritting my teeth together hard. "Thanks." Time to change the subject. "Hey, do you two want to go tobogganing sometime soon? This weekend, maybe?"

"Yeah, that'd be cool," Victoria said.

"I'm in too," Felicia agreed, smiling.

I pictured the tobogganing hills outside town. The snow would be perfect after all this cold weather. "I bet I could talk my mom into driving us," I said. She didn't usually volunteer on the weekend, and she couldn't paint *all* the time. I imagined the three of us piling into the back of our old car. Newsflash: Cassidy Silver has friends. Who would have guessed that it was possible?

I had to admit it. It felt good. Really good.

"Hey, Cassie." Ben's voice interrupted my thoughts.

"Hey, Ben." My heart sank. How was I supposed to have friends if I always had to walk my brother home? "How about you go on ahead and I'll catch up?"

Ben hesitated; then he gave a small nod.

"You sure you're okay with that?" I asked, trying not to sound impatient.

"I'm not a baby, Cassidy. I'll be fine." Ben adjusted his backpack over his shoulder and set off. Relieved, I turned back to the others.

"Yeah, Ms. Allyson is great," Felicia was saying to Victoria. "Remember Mr. McMaran? I'm so glad he's gone."

"Yeah, I just started here right before he left, but he seemed pretty awful," Victoria said, straight-faced.

I wondered how Victoria managed to keep her secret. If it was me, I'd be dying to tell Felicia—to tell everyone, actually—that I was the one who got rid of Mr. McMaran. She'd be the school hero. If, of course, anyone believed her. I studied her face and wished I knew for sure. With every day that passed, the more impossible it all seemed.

I guess I sort of lost track of time while we talked, because when I finally glanced at my watch, it was close to four o'clock. "Oh, wow, look at the time! How did that happen? I've got to run, I told Ben I'd catch up with him." I took off, sprinting out of the schoolyard and down the sidewalk, my feet slipping a little on the icy surface. A man with a shaved head crossed the street in front of me and my heart skipped a beat. Then he turned his head toward me, and I could see it wasn't Rick. It left me feeling unsettled all the same. Maybe Victoria should have told her parents that Rick was hanging around the school. Still, it was her decision, not mine.

Anyway, I had bigger problems right now. It was Thursday, which meant Mom would be at home, painting. And I couldn't see Ben anywhere.

Fourteen

By the time I got in the front door, I was breathing hard and sweating under my winter coat. I untied my boots and pulled them off, scattering wet clumps of snow across the tiled floor of the front hall.

"Cassidy?" Mom called from the kitchen. Her voice was all tight, the way it gets when she's angry.

"I'm sorry, Mom. I was just…" I walked into the kitchen and stopped dead. Ben was sitting on Mom's lap, his face against her shoulder and his skinny shoulders shaking with sobs. When he heard my voice, he lifted his head and looked at me for a second; then he turned away, avoiding my eyes. The left side of his face was red and raw-looking and blood was smeared on his lip and chin.

My heart thudded painfully in my chest. "What happened?" I blurted. "Tyler Patterson! Did he hit you?"

Mom looked at me like I was a stranger. "Go to your room, Cassidy. I don't want to talk to you right now."

"I'm sorry, Mom!"

"Ben's the one you should be saying sorry to," she said. "Go to your room. I'll talk to you later."

I backed slowly out of the room, ran up the stairs and threw myself onto my bed. It wasn't fair. Tyler Patterson. Amber's brother. He was the one Mom should be angry with, not me. Okay, I was supposed to walk Ben home, but why was it always my job to take care of Ben? Why couldn't Mom meet him after school herself? If she wasn't always so busy, maybe she'd have known Ben was being bullied and done something about it by now. Then this would never have happened.

I pictured Ben's face and started to cry. I pushed my face into my pillow and sobbed until I was all out of tears, dizzy and aching and empty.

Eventually Mom called me downstairs. I didn't want to go. I sat on the edge of my bed and stared at the hats and scarves hanging on my wall. Mom didn't understand anything. She didn't even know that the last year of school had been torture, or that things had just started to look more hopeful. She didn't have time to hear about my life at all. And now she was furious with me for letting Ben down.

I dragged myself downstairs, my stomach in knots. Ben was curled up on the family room couch with a soft quilt and a mug of hot chocolate. He was sucking his thumb.

I hadn't seen him do that for a really long time, and my anger instantly faded. "I'm sorry," I said softly.

Ben pulled his thumb out of his mouth and quickly shoved his hand under the quilt. "It's okay, Cassie. I told Mom it wasn't your fault." He gave me a tiny smile. "I didn't mean to get you in trouble."

"I deserve it. I shouldn't have let you go ahead." I swallowed hard, remembering what he'd said before about getting picked on because I was his sister. "I only wanted to talk to my friends for a few minutes," I told him. "I never thought anything would happen to you."

"Tyler hates me," he said. His eyes were puffy from crying. "He says he's gonna pound me."

I swallowed, feeling helpless. I didn't know what to say. Amber might hate me and she could be pretty mean—but she used words, not fists.

Ben looked down at the quilt and started picking at a loose thread. "Mom wants to talk to you," he said. "She's in the kitchen."

Mom was making chili for dinner, a pot steaming and bubbling on the stove. She was actually cooking. I wondered if that meant she was feeling guilty about Ben too. I frowned. A pot of chili wasn't going to fix anything.

"I just wanted to talk to my friends for a few minutes," I told her. "I didn't mean to stay so long."

She kept stirring the pot. "I'm disappointed in you, Cassidy. I don't think it's a lot to ask you to walk home with Ben."

I swallowed hard. I didn't want to start crying. "He said he'd be okay."

"Of course he said he'd be okay." Mom looked exasperated. "Ben looks up to you."

I stared at her. "He does?"

"He's been following you around since he learned how to walk." Mom turned down the stove and started slicing mushrooms, the knife clicking fast against the wooden cutting board. "It's not easy for him to make friends. He's not as confident as you."

"Me? Confident?"

She sighed. "You've always had lots of friends, but Ben isn't like you. We don't ask you to look after him very often. I need to be able to trust you to take care of him when we do."

"What friends?" I raised my voice. "Hello? Mom, where have you been for the last year?"

"What are you talking about?"

I was almost shouting now. I couldn't help it. "I'm talking about everyone making fun of my lisp, and Chiaki dumping me, and me having no friends at all. I'm talking about being Cathidy Thilver, the school freak. Okay? Satisfied?"

Mom looked stunned. "Cassidy, are you serious? I knew you and Chiaki didn't spend much time together anymore, but I assumed you'd just drifted apart. I had no idea."

I stared at the counter. "Yeah, well, you've been busy."

Mom reached out a hand toward me. "Not too busy for you, honey. I'd never be too busy for you."

I pulled away and shrugged. "Could've fooled me." I didn't meet her eyes. There was a long tense silence; then I changed the subject. "Mom," I whispered, "did Tyler hit him?"

She sighed and let her hand drop back to her side. "No, Tyler and some other boys were calling him names and throwing snowballs at him. Ben was running away and he fell. His lip got cut on his bottom teeth, but he'll be fine."

I fiddled with a mushroom, peeling off its thin translucent skin and watching it blur through my tears. "Mom, I really am sorry."

"Oh, honey." She put down the knife. "I know you are." She slid the chopping board across the counter to me. "Here, chop some peppers for me."

I chopped peppers ferociously. If only there was something I could do. Ben was so smart that sometimes I forgot how young he was. I mean, this was the kid who would help me with my math homework when I got stuck. I remembered him sitting on Mom's lap, his face covered in blood, and I felt a surge of hot anger. How could Tyler and his friends do this to him? I wished there was some way I could get even.

If Victoria was telling me the truth—if telekinesis was real and if I could learn it—then maybe I could.

Fifteen

The deadline for the art contest was sneaking up fast. Only a week to go, and what had I done? Squat. Zero. Zilch. All around me, the classroom was filled with people painting, sketching, sculpting and gluing. Then there was me. I had nothing that resembled an art project: just my notebook of scribbling. I flipped back to the beginning. *Who is Cassidy Silver?* I'd written pages and pages, but I wasn't sure I was any closer to an answer.

Ms. Allyson appeared beside me. She had a way of doing that—you'd think those red cowboy boots would be kind of clunky on the hard floor, but she walked lightly. She looked a bit like a dancer, I thought. I wished I was graceful like that.

"I like your T-shirt," she said.

I glanced down. I was wearing a very old and faded T-shirt that said *Nobody Knows I'm Elvis.* "You do?"

"I'm a big Elvis fan," she admitted. "Don't spread it around."

I laughed. "Your secret is safe with me."

"So, how is the art project going?"

I shrugged. "I sort of got stuck. Then I thought writing would get me unstuck but, well, now I seem to be stuck in writing."

"Hmmm. Have you tried collage? There're several boxes of magazines just waiting to be cut up. You could take a look through them, see if some of the images call out to you."

"Sure. It's not like I have any better ideas."

Ms. Allyson laughed. "Oh, dear. You do sound discouraged."

"It's, um, I just seem to have a bit too much on my mind. Or something." I didn't know quite why I'd said that and I started backpedaling. "I mean, I'm fine. It's nothing major, just sort of busy."

"Uh-huh." She started to walk toward a student who was waving a frantic hand. "Give collage a try," she said over her shoulder.

I nodded and headed over to the art supply corner. It wasn't Ms. Allyson I wanted to talk to. It was my mother. And I couldn't help thinking that winning the contest would make things between Mom and me better somehow. I'd told her about getting teased and about Chiaki and everything, and she hadn't even mentioned it again. She'd just gone right back to having no time for me.

I sighed, picked up a box of magazines and started flipping through the pages. Trees, faces, animals, cars.

Images that call out to you, Ms. Allyson had said. If any images were calling out to me, they were doing it too quietly for me to hear. I sighed again. I really didn't like art very much.

I wanted to ask Victoria if she'd seen Rick again, but Felicia joined us at lunch and I didn't like to bring it up with her there. Instead I told them both about what had happened to Ben the day before.

"Tyler Patterson!" Felicia wrinkled her snub nose. "Is he Amber's brother?"

"It figures, huh?"

She nodded. "I wonder why those two are so mean."

I shrugged. "Who cares why? They're both bullies and they're probably going to grow up to be bigger bullies."

"Like Mr. McMaran," Victoria added.

I imagined Amber wearing Mr. McMaran's old suit and reading a cigar magazine. "Yuck. Imagine having Amber as a teacher. At least we'll all be long gone by then."

Felicia started to laugh. Then she stopped, frowning. "It's awful about your brother," she said. "Is your mom going to call the school?"

"I don't think so."

"She should," Victoria said. "There's got to be something the school could do."

"There's a zero tolerance program for bullying," I said. "I totally think Mom should call Mrs. Goldstein, but Ben begged her not to. He says if Tyler knows he told on him, it would make it worse."

"Yeah, it probably would." Felicia looked away, staring down at the ground.

I wondered if she was thinking about her own experiences. "It sucks, doesn't it? I mean, Ben gets picked on because he's small and smart." And because he's my brother. I pushed the thought aside. "And me, because of the stupid lisp, and Victoria, because she's new, and Nathan, probably because he's the only black kid in the whole school, and…"

Felicia finished my sentence. "And me, because I'm fat."

"You're not fat," I said automatically.

"I am though. I mean, I know you're trying to be nice, but it's a fact." She looked at me. "I've always been overweight. My whole family is." She grinned. "Mom and I have started going to the gym together."

"I think you look fine." I did too. She had a round pretty face with huge dark eyes and a wide full-lipped smile and masses of gorgeous, curly, black hair.

"Thanks," she said. "I sort of think I do too. But it's hard, hearing the stuff Amber says all the time."

"Tell me about it," I agreed.

Felicia raised her eyebrows. "You look like it rolls right off you. Like you couldn't care less what Amber says. Honestly, I think you intimidate her."

I rolled my eyes. "I'm a good actor," I said. "I don't want to give Amber the satisfaction of knowing she bothers me." I thought about it for a moment. "You know, now that we're all friends, it doesn't really bother me so much."

"At least Amber doesn't threaten to hit people," Victoria said. "Poor Ben. Did you get in a lot of trouble from your mom?"

I made a face. "She was pretty upset at first."

"But you're not grounded or anything?"

"No, Mom doesn't really do that." I thought I'd prefer it if she did. I could still hear her saying she was disappointed in me, and that was far worse than a simple punishment would have been. "I'm trying to think of a way to get back at Tyler and his friends," I said. I gave Victoria a meaningful look, hoping she'd understand.

"What can you do?" Felicia asked. "I mean, if you talk to Tyler, he'll take it out on Ben."

"I hate bullies." Victoria closed her eyes for a moment, as if she was thinking hard. When she opened them again, she was looking right at me.

My heart leapt. The last time she'd said that she'd been talking about McMoron. I didn't want to say anything about telekinesis in front of Felicia. "Maybe we can do something about it," I said carefully.

Felicia shrugged. "I don't see what."

"No." Victoria met my eyes for a second; then she dropped her gaze and her cheeks turned pink. "I don't either."

Sixteen

Ben and I were standing side by side at the sink, washing the dishes from dinner, when he suddenly crashed a saucepan down on the counter and turned to me.

"Cassidy, can I talk to you about something?" he asked.

"Sure." I hoped it wasn't about what had happened yesterday. I couldn't look at his bruised face without feeling guilty.

"It's about Tyler Patterson."

"What about him?"

"He grabbed me in the hallway today and called me a little nerd. He says he's going to get me." Ben's voice wobbled, and he dropped it to a barely audible whisper. "Cassie, I'm scared of him."

"Maybe you should talk to Mom," I suggested. Even as I said it, I knew he wouldn't.

"I can't." Ben's eyes filled with tears and his lower lip trembled. "If she knows I'm scared, she'll call the school for sure."

"Well, maybe she should. Tyler shouldn't get away with this kind of bullying."

Ben shook his head vehemently. "No way. If Tyler finds out I told, he'll slaughter me. Seriously."

I stared into the soapy water, trying to make a decision. "Look," I said finally, "I think I might have an idea. I need to make a phone call. Can you finish up the dishes?"

He looked at me sceptically. "What kind of idea?"

"I can't tell you yet. But let me see what I can do, okay?" I rushed up to my room, sat down on my bed and held my breath for a moment. I didn't want to make Victoria mad. But she'd said she hated bullies. And what was the point in having these powers if you never used them? If she really was my friend, and if she really was telekinetic, she had to help Ben.

I dialed her number. The phone rang and rang. *Pick up, pick up.* As soon as she answered, I jumped right in. "It's me, Cassidy. Listen, Victoria. You know what we were talking about at school? About bullying and what happened to Ben?"

"Yeah."

"Well, he's pretty scared. Tyler's been threatening him."

"Jeez. Poor little guy."

"Yeah." I hesitated. "I was thinking, couldn't you help him?"

"Me? How?"

"You know. Do some tricks or something to scare Tyler. Like you did to Mr. McMaran. Maybe if we set it up so that he thought Ben was doing it?"

Victoria cut in. "No. You know I can't."

"Why not?" My voice came out sounding sharper than I meant it to.

"I promised my mom. I told you that. I'm not allowed to do that stuff at all."

"Yeah, but this is different. This is really important." I stood up and paced a few steps to my dresser. My reflection stared back at me from the mirror. "You did it that other time. With Mr. McMaran."

There was a long pause.

"Victoria? You did do that, right?"

She sighed into the phone. "Yeah, but I shouldn't have. I just got really mad."

"And what happened to Ben doesn't make you mad?"

"It does," she protested. "But I can't do anything about it. Please don't ask me to."

Her tone warned me to back off, but I couldn't stop myself. "Just this once. Why can't you do it once more to help Ben?"

"Cassidy, please stop. I don't want to talk about this."

I stared at my reflection and twisted a lock of hair around my finger. My heart was beating fast, and I couldn't stop the words from tumbling out: "Maybe you won't help because you're not really telekinetic."

There was an awful silence. I wished I could snatch the words back, but it was too late. They hung sharp and heavy between us, threatening to ruin everything.

"I have to go," Victoria said flatly.

I blinked back tears. "No, Victoria. Wait. I didn't mean it."

Click. I listened to the dial tone for a minute. I felt like hurling the phone across the room, but instead I set it carefully back on its stand. Then I sat down on my bed, cross-legged, pressed my hands together like Victoria had shown me, and took some slow deep breaths. *Visualize the energy.*

If Victoria wouldn't help Ben—or couldn't help Ben—I'd have to do it myself.

All that evening I practiced. I sat on the floor in my room, visualizing energy and trying to form it into a ball between my hands. I placed a pencil on the floor and willed it to move. I even looked up telekinesis on the Internet. I figured I could say that it was for a school project if Ben or Mom noticed. I didn't find anything helpful. Just once, for a few seconds, I thought I could feel the energy growing denser between my hands, but it dissipated before I could be certain. It was like trying to grasp a sunbeam.

At least it took all my concentration, which meant I couldn't think about Victoria and whether I'd just wrecked our friendship. *I'm glad you trust me,* I'd told her. What were the chances of her trusting me after what I'd said? I shook my head hard and tried to focus. *Green ball of energy...*

After a couple of hours, Mom poked her head into my room. I jumped off the bed, startled. I didn't want to have to explain what I was doing.

"Is everything all right?" she asked.

"Yeah, I guess."

"You've been hiding out in your room all evening." She frowned. "That's not like you."

I was surprised she'd noticed.

"Look, I know I've been busy lately." Mom stepped into my room. She was wearing her painting things and she looked tired. "The other day you said you felt like I'd been too busy. Like I didn't have time for you." She cleared her throat. "If you want to talk...but you never do, Cassidy. You always say everything's fine. If I ask if you're okay, you snap at me or push me away." She lifted her hands, palms up, in a helpless shrug. "I don't know what you want me to do."

I stared at her. I didn't know what to say. If I started talking, I didn't know what would come out. How was I supposed to talk to her about getting bugged by kids at school when she spent practically every evening at the hospice talking to people who were dying? How was I supposed to tell her that I couldn't even come up with a project for the art contest when she was this amazing artist?

I couldn't tell her about the telekinesis, so I couldn't tell her about the fight I'd had with Victoria. It was my fault Ben was in trouble, so I couldn't talk about that either.

Mom shrugged. "See? I try, but you don't seem to want to talk to me. I don't know what else to do." She turned to leave.

I didn't want her to go. I wanted to run after her and tell her everything. "Mom!"

She slowly turned around to face me. "Cassidy."

"Umm. Will you take me and some friends tobogganing tomorrow?" I crossed my fingers that Victoria would still want to come. I couldn't blame her if she stayed mad. I'd as good as called her a liar.

Mom sighed. "Sure, Cassidy. No problem."

Seventeen

I called Felicia first, since she didn't have any reason to be mad at me.

"I'm in!" she said immediately.

I figured that she probably hadn't had a whole lot of invitations lately. Like in the last couple of years. "Great. Cool. We'll pick you up in the morning, okay?"

"Okay. Victoria's coming too?"

I carefully kept my anxiety out of my voice. "Don't know yet. I have to call her."

"Oh, she'll come," Felicia said confidently. "She was all over the idea."

I hoped she was right.

Victoria picked up the phone on the first ring. "Rick, I told you not call."

"Victoria? It's me. Cassidy." Her words slowly registered. "Has Rick been calling you?"

Victoria's voice was cool and careful. "Cassidy? What do you want?"

"Look, I'm thorry." I winced. "*Sorry.* I'm an idiot, okay? A total jerk. I deserve to be voted off the island. No—worse than that. I deserve to be stuck on an island with Amber and Madeline. I shouldn't have said that to you, and I shouldn't have even thought it, and I'm really, really thorry. *Sorry.*"

There was a long pause. I bit my lip and waited. *Please still be my friend.* I could hear her breathing too close to the phone. "It's okay," she said at last. "I guess that's why I've never told anyone before. I figured no one would believe it."

"I do believe you," I said. Then I added, more honestly, "I mean, I don't think you would lie to me. Telekinesis, well, it's a hard thing to accept, you know? I spent hours trying to do it tonight, and I wouldn't have done that if I really thought you were making it up."

"Yeah." Her voice was a bit thick-sounding, like she'd been crying.

"Are you okay?" I remembered how she'd answered the phone. "Hey—did Rick phone you? What was that about?"

"He called," she said. "Tonight, right after I got off the phone with you. I thought it was you calling back, so I picked up right away. Just as well. If Mom had answered..." She made a funny choking sound, like she was holding back tears. "I can't stand it. I mean, I've met you and Felicia, and everything is going so well here. I don't want Rick to mess everything up again."

"What did he call for? I mean, what did he say?"

"Oh, same old, same old. He's got this crazy idea that he could make all kinds of money if I'd help him." She hesitated. "He didn't come right out and say this, but I think he's got himself into trouble of some kind. He said he owes a lot of money."

"Like, to a drug dealer or something?"

"I don't know. Probably, yeah. Anyway, he wouldn't listen to me. I told him that it wouldn't work anyway. We'd just get caught, and we'd both be in a ton of trouble."

"So, did he…?"

"He hung up. Then you called back, and I thought it was him."

"Jeez."

"Yeah, if he calls and Mom or Dad picks up the phone…"

"Maybe you should tell them," I said. "I mean, if you're scared of him."

"You think I should?"

I hesitated. "I don't know," I said at last. "It's up to you."

"I don't know," she wailed. "I don't know what to do."

Mom would know what to do, I thought suddenly. Mom dealt with problems bigger than this. She talked to suicidal people on the crisis line, people who were really lost and scared and alone. She'd be able to figure this out somehow. And, well, it had sounded like she actually did want me to talk to her about stuff. "Victoria? Can I ask my mom? Or, I don't know, do you want to talk to her, maybe?"

"No. No, don't tell anyone, okay? Promise."

"I promise." I sucked on my bottom lip, wondering what to do. Then I remembered the other reason I had called. "Hey, want to go tobogganing tomorrow? Mom says she'll drive, and Felicia says she's in."

"I'm in too! Well, I should check with my parents, but I'm sure they'll let me." She lowered her voice. "They've been fighting all night. It's awful. I'll be glad to get out of the house for the day."

"Um, Victoria? Do they fight a lot?"

She didn't answer right away. When she spoke, her voice was flat. "All the time," she said. "All the time."

I swallowed. When Dad's home, he and Mom are like a couple of teenagers, always kissing and giggling and stuff. It's embarrassing, but I wouldn't change it. "You can always come here," I said. "We'd be happy to have you over whenever you want. Dinner, sleepovers, whatever. Mom says our friends are always welcome, as long as they don't expect anything fancy."

"Thanks," Victoria said. "You're a good friend, Cassidy."

When I'm not accusing you of lying, I thought guiltily. "So are you," I told her. "My best friend."

Eighteen

The next morning dawned clear and icy cold, with a hard pale sun and a cloudless blue sky. There were tons of kids already on the hill when we arrived. We all scrambled out of Mom's station wagon with my wooden toboggan and Ben's flying saucer, and a tiny blue-hatted girl came flying across the parking lot to meet us.

"Sydney's here?" I asked, stating the obvious.

Ben grinned at me. "Sure. You didn't think I was going to hang out with you, did you?"

I laughed. "As a matter of fact…"

And the two of them were gone, racing up the hill side by side.

Felicia appeared to be frozen to the spot, staring after them. "It's awfully steep," she said.

I squinted up at the hill. The glare of the snow was blinding. To the left of the run, a line of kids trudged up the slope, toboggans tucked under their arms or being tugged along behind them. They looked like ants, steadily working their way up, up, up, single file. I shook my head and started walking. "This is the best hill," I told her, leading the way. "We call it the Demolition Demon, because it's so fast."

She didn't move.

"You're not scared, are you?" I asked her. "Because it's just a joke, the demolition thing. It's not really that steep."

"I've never tobogganed before," she admitted. "We didn't get much snow where we used to live."

Victoria grinned and took her arm. "First time for everything."

From the top, I had to admit it looked awfully cliff-like.

"Are you sure you want to do this?" I asked Felicia. "Because if you're nervous…"

Victoria laughed. "Don't tell me the fearless Cassidy is scared."

I rolled my eyes. "Whatever."

They both giggled.

"I am so not scared," I told them firmly. I sat down on my old-fashioned wooden sled. "Coming with me? There's lots of room."

Victoria sat down at the back and gestured to Felicia to sit in the middle. Felicia hesitated, her dark eyes wide and anxious; then she squeezed in, wrapping her arms tightly around my waist.

"Ready?"

"Ready!"

And we were off, flying down the hill so fast the wind whipped my hair back, made my eyes water and blew the tears off my face. The wind stole the breath right out of my lungs.

"That was awesome," Victoria gasped when we finally slid to a stop. "Let's do it again."

I twisted around. "Felicia? All right?"

"Fabulous." She laughed. "Incredible."

We scrambled to our feet and, dragging the toboggan behind us, started back up the hill.

The runs got faster as the morning went on. The weight of hundreds of kids careening down had packed the snow and made it smooth and icy.

"One more time," Felicia panted as we trudged up the hill, pulling the toboggan behind us. "Then I need a break. This is worse than going to the gym."

I laughed. "But you're doing it with us instead of your mom. Doesn't that count for something?"

"My turn to go in front," Victoria announced, plunking herself down. Felicia and I sat down behind her and we were off, laughing. Next thing I knew the sled was twisting sideways and I was flying through the air. *Oof.* I hit the ground, rolled a few times and landed face down at the bottom of the hill. A second later,

Victoria landed on top of me. I spluttered, my mouth full of snow.

Victoria rolled off and lay beside me. Felicia had landed a few feet away and she came crawling over to join us.

"Tobogganing," she muttered. "And here I thought you guys liked me."

I couldn't stop laughing. I rolled onto one elbow to watch my friends. Felicia's hat had flown off and her dark hair was tangled and full of ice. Victoria's face was lit up, long curving dimples framing her mouth, those pink gums and white teeth showing in a grin so wide it looked totally goofy. I didn't care if she was really telekinetic or not, I decided. I didn't always understand her, but she was my friend and that was all there was to it.

"Cassidy! Come quick!" Sydney appeared beside us, breathing hard, like she had been running.

I scrambled to my feet. "What is it? Is Ben okay?"

Sydney shook her head and swallowed a sob. "Tyler… he's here with his friends. And they've got Ben."

I jumped to my feet, abandoning the toboggan, and followed Sydney, tearing along the foot of the hill. I could hear Victoria and Felicia running behind me, their boots crunching in the packed snow.

Sydney led us past the tobogganing area and over to the half-frozen creek that ran along the base of the hill. My heart was beating hard. A kid had drowned here a few years ago. The story was that he had fallen through the ice and been swept under by the current. I didn't know if it was true or not, but no one was allowed to toboggan on this part of the hill anymore. We ran along the side of the creek, past the parking lot, until the creek turned and disappeared into the woods.

"They were right here a minute ago." Sydney twisted her hands together anxiously. "Where would they have gone?"

It was surprisingly quiet down by the stream. The screams and laughter of the kids on the hill sounded muffled and distant. I could hear the gurgling of icy water flowing fast under a thin crust of ice. I stood silent for a moment, listening. A startled bird flew out of the trees.

"Did you hear anything?" I asked.

Sydney shook her head, but Felicia was pointing into the woods. "Maybe?"

I started running again, into the trees, in the direction the bird had come from. In a couple of minutes I saw Ben, perched precariously on a rock, leaning over the icy stream, reaching as far as he could with a long stick held in his hand.

I ran toward him. "Careful!" I grabbed the back of his jacket tightly. My heart was banging like crazy. "What are you doing?"

"My hat!" Ben pointed.

I followed his gaze. His red wool hat was in the water, caught on some branches and just out of reach.

"I'll get it. My arms are longer." I took the stick from him and helped him off the rock to more secure footing. For a kid who was supposed to be a genius, he sure could be dumb sometimes. He didn't seem to have a clue how dangerous the half-frozen stream was.

Ben tucked his bare hands under his arms. "Thanks." He started crying, and Sydney put her arms around him.

I managed to hook the hat with the stick and, with some difficulty, pulled it free of the branches it was snagged on. I dropped the sodden mass on the snow beside me and looked ruefully at Ben. "It won't do you much good like that."

Ben made a funny choking sound, like he didn't know whether to laugh or cry. "No," he said.

"Where are your mittens?" asked Sydney. She tugged his hands out from his armpits and looked at them. They were red and raw-looking. "You're gonna get frostbite."

"Tyler threw them in the stream."

I stared at the cold water rushing by. Ben's mittens were probably miles downstream by now.

"Everyone knows how dangerous this stream is. If you had fallen in…" I shook my head slowly. "What is Tyler's problem?"

Ben shrugged. "He says I talk like a freak."

"Just because you use words of more than one syllable," said Sydney indignantly. "Tyler is an imbecile. He doesn't know what Ben means half the time, and it makes him mad."

I looked at Victoria and Felicia. "What should we do? Mom's not picking us up for another hour."

Victoria didn't answer. She met my eyes, frowning; then she quickly looked away.

I caught my breath. "Can you guys excuse us a moment?" I grabbed her arm and pulled her aside. "So?"

She shook her head and spoke in an urgent whisper. "No, I know what you're going to say and the answer's no. I want to, I really do, but I can't. I—"

"Promised your mom," I finished. "I know, but Victoria, this is really serious. I mean, a kid drowned in that creek a few years ago. We can't let Tyler get away with this."

"I'm not saying we should let him get away with it."

"What then?"

She shook her head. "I don't know."

I stared at the ground. I didn't want to fight with her again, but I couldn't help being angry. What was the use of having this incredible power if she wouldn't use it? "What if Ben had fallen in?" I asked. "Would you have used your power to get him out or would you just let him drown?"

My words came out sounding harsher than I meant them to. Victoria's cheeks flushed as pink as if I'd slapped her. She was quiet for a moment. "I'd have jumped in myself if I had to," she said. Her voice was so sad I could hardly stand it.

It didn't make any sense, but I could have sworn she looked ashamed. "Victoria…"

"If it wasn't for me, Rick wouldn't have gone to jail and my parents wouldn't always be fighting." Her voice broke. "You think it's so great being telekinetic? You don't understand anything."

Nineteen

Sydney was watching us impatiently. "Look, I'm sorry to interrupt but…"

I turned back to her. "We're trying to figure out what to do, okay? If Victoria would help…"

"She can't," Sydney said flatly.

"What do you mean, she can't?"

Sydney gave me an exasperated look. "I mean, if you guys just fix things for Ben today, it won't change anything. It'll just be the same tomorrow, and you can't always be there."

I folded my arms across my chest. "So, what are you suggesting, Sydney? We all give up and go home?"

"Maybe we should," Ben said. He sounded defeated. "Maybe we should find someone who has a cell phone and call Mom."

Sydney stamped her foot. "Ben, don't be a wimp."

I scowled at her. "I thought you were his friend."

"I am," she said. "And if you really want to help him,

you have to help him figure out how to do this on his own."

For a skinny little kid, she sure had a lot of opinions. There was a long silence. Felicia and Victoria both stared at Sydney; then slowly they both turned and looked at me.

Finally Felicia spoke. "It's not like we don't have some experience with bullies," she pointed out. "Um, Ben? I don't know if you already know this, but I've been picked on a fair bit by Tyler's sister, Amber."

"We all have," I said. "We all know what it's like."

"She doesn't threaten to beat you up," Ben pointed out.

I nodded. "True. But you know what? You have to make Tyler think he doesn't scare you."

"But he does scare me," Ben said. "I'd be an idiot not to be scared of him. He's twice my size, and he likes to hit people."

"Ben's got a point," Victoria admitted.

"I didn't say he shouldn't be scared. I said that he had to pretend he wasn't scared." I thought about Amber. "It's different."

"I'm not such a good actor," Ben said.

I glared at him. "Well, you're about to get better, okay?"

He nodded, wide-eyed, and I suddenly remembered what Mom had said about him looking up to me. "Listen, Ben." I hesitated; then I plunged on. "I've been scared of Amber. I mean, I know she hasn't threatened to beat me up, but I've been scared, okay? So I do understand."

"Okay," he whispered.

"And you know what? It's so not okay, what Tyler's doing to you."

"That's right," Sydney said, nodding. "That's what I keep telling him."

"So let's go have a word with him." I nodded in the direction of the hill. "Come on."

Ben's shoulders slumped. "Cassie, I think I want to go home."

I didn't know how hard to push him. "It's up to you," I said finally. "But if you just give up, this stuff is going to keep happening."

Felicia looked at him, her face serious. "It's not just you, you know. Tyler bullies other kids too. If you let him go on doing this, nothing's going to change."

"Other kids?" Ben looked startled. "Are you sure?"

She nodded. "Absolutely."

There was a long silence. Ben shrugged helplessly. "I guess it can't make things much worse." He rubbed his eyes, brushing away tears. "What do you want me to do?"

"I'll start," I said. "Just act like you're not scared, okay? And when it's your turn, stand up for yourself."

We all trooped back up to the top of the toboggan run and waited for Tyler. Finally we saw him. He was flanked by two other boys and they were hauling a huge black inner tube behind them.

Victoria reached out and grasped Ben's shoulder. "Ready?"

Ben shook his head. "No, I don't know. I don't think I can do this." His chin was trembling.

"It'll be okay," I said softly, hoping I was right. "We won't let them hurt you."

"Cassie, please." Ben's shoulders hunched up. "I can't do this."

I wanted to hug him but not with Tyler watching. I let my arms fall back to my sides, and I looked Ben straight in the eyes.

"Ben, don't let being scared stop you."

Ben nodded mutely.

"You know what?" I said. "I was going to call Tyler over for a word, but it'd be even better if you did it."

I didn't really think he would do it, but he stood up and took a shaky step toward the older boys. He looked terrified. I could hardly stand it.

"Hey, Tyler!" Ben called out. His voice shook a little.

Tyler spun around. "Well, if it isn't the little freak. Too bad. I was hoping you'd fall in the crick and drown."

I couldn't believe this fourth grader had the nerve to say that in front of the five of us. I wanted to pick him up and shake him until what little brain matter he had was completely scrambled.

Tyler laughed. "Hiding behind a bunch of girls, nerd-boy?"

I squeezed Ben's shoulder, and he stepped forward. "I'm not hiding behind anyone," he said. "And I'm not scared of you. You're just a bully. And you know what?" His voice got stronger. "Most bullies have low self-esteem."

I didn't know quite what I'd expected him to say but that wasn't it. I wondered where he was going with it.

Tyler stared at him. "What are you talking about?"

"I read a book about it," Ben said. He sounded more confident now that he was talking about something he'd read. "Most bullies are actually insecure and just trying to make themselves feel better by—"

"Shut up," Tyler said. "Your sister and your girl-friend aren't always going to be around to protect you, you know."

Felicia stepped toward him. "But you know what? He'll tell us. And we know where to find you."

"What are you gonna do, fatty? Sit on me?"

Felicia didn't even flinch. "If necessary," she said grimly.

Sydney put her arm around Ben. "Ben has lots of friends, Tyler. And we don't like people who hurt him."

"Just leave me alone, Tyler." Ben's voice wobbled slightly. "I don't do anything to bother you."

"You breathe," Tyler said. "That bothers me. Your stupid face bothers me."

My heart was beating so hard and fast I felt like it might explode. I had to say something. "You're the stupid one,"

I told Tyler. "What's your problem, anyway? How come you're such a little jerk?"

Tyler stared at me, taken aback for a second.

I made a loud buzzer noise. "Game over. You lose."

But Tyler wasn't backing down. He turned back to Ben. "Look, nerd-boy. You don't tell me what to do. Your friends don't tell me what to do. Some time, it'll just be you and me and then?" He smacked one fist into his other hand. "Pow."

"Nice gloves," Victoria said. "I think you owe Ben a pair."

"That's right," I said. "You want to hand them over, or should we come and get them?"

For the first time, Tyler looked uncertain. "You wouldn't."

I shrugged. "Well, not if you'd rather I called your mom and told her that you threw Ben's in the creek."

Tyler took a step back. "You can't do that!"

Aha. Finally. We'd found a crack. I nudged Ben to make sure he'd noticed.

Ben smiled. "Well, I'm sure she'd want to know."

No dummy, my little brother.

Tyler pulled his gloves off and threw them at Ben. "Fine. I hate these stupid gloves anyway."

Ben picked them up and put them on. "Leather. Nice."

He looked like he'd just grown about six inches. There were all kinds of things I wanted to say to Tyler, but I thought I'd let Ben take it from here.

"Tyler." Ben gave him a long look. "There's a program at school that might interest you."

Tyler snorted. "I doubt that."

"It's an anti-bullying program. Zero-tolerance. You know what that means?"

Sydney nudged me, beaming delightedly. "I've been talking to him about this for ages!" she whispered.

"Whatever," Tyler said. He turned to walk away.

"If you ever hit me—or even threaten me, or chase me, or call me names—again, I'm going to tell. I'll tell our teacher. I'll tell the principal." Ben raised his voice. "And I'll tell your mother."

For a moment I thought we'd won.

Then Tyler took a step toward us. "Sure you will." He lifted his chin and stared at Ben with hard eyes. "Remember what I said. Sometime soon, when it's just the two of us?" He punched his fist into his hand again. "You're dead, kid."

Twenty

For the next few days, I didn't let Ben out of my sight on the way to and from school. I was worried that I'd made things worse by encouraging him to take a stand. I couldn't keep an eye on him all the time, and what would happen if Tyler caught him alone? Sitting at my desk, I clenched my fists and felt helpless.

I pushed my worries aside and tried to concentrate. The art project was due the next day, and what did I have? A bunch of cut up magazines and a spiral-bound journal full of scribbled notes about myself. *Who is Cassidy Silver?* Not an artist, clearly. Still, I had to hand in something. I flipped through my pile of magazine cuttings and looked around the classroom to see who was hogging all the glue sticks.

Joe Cicarelli appeared to have three. I wandered over to his desk and held out my hand. "Got a spare glue stick, Joe?"

He picked one up. "It'll cost ya."

"Cost me what?"

He nodded at my T-shirt. I glanced down at it. Light green with black letters: *What would Scooby Doo?*

"You want my T-shirt? For a glue stick?" I snorted. "No way."

He laughed. "Nah. I just want to know where you get them."

I grinned. "Ah, well. That's top secret information. It'll cost you at least two glue sticks."

He reluctantly handed over another one. "So much for my art project. I was going to make a glue stick sculpture and now you've ruined it."

"How exactly would a glue stick sculpture reflect who you are? You have some obsession with glue sticks or something?"

Joe clutched one hand to his heart. "I'm wounded. Cut to the quick." Then he frowned. "It's supposed to be about me? I missed that part."

"Oh, boy. Look, because I feel sorry for you, I'll let you in on my secret." I leaned over and wrote the address for my favorite T-shirt website on one of the scraps of construction paper littering his desk. "There you go. Enjoy." I headed back to my desk, two glue sticks richer and smiling to myself. School was a lot more fun than it used to be.

Half an hour later, I had something to hand in. I just wasn't sure it counted as an art project. I glanced around the room. Victoria looked like she was deep in concentration over her project, so I wandered over to say hi to Felicia and Nathan. One of the best things about art was that Ms. Allyson let us move about and talk to each other during class.

Nathan grinned. "Hey, so are you getting somewhere?"

"I'm done," I said smugly. Then I sighed and made a face. "Actually, I just cut some stuff up and stuck it together. I've decided that art isn't one of my strengths." I tried not to think about how great it would've been to tell my mom that I'd won an art contest.

"Want to see mine?" Nathan asked, sliding his painting toward me.

"Wow. That's totally cool." It looked like it had started out as a collage of black and white images—photographs, mostly of trees and fences and snow—but he'd painted over top so that the images were stained with color.

"I took all the photographs myself," he said. "Developed them and everything at home."

"Seriously?"

"It's kind of a hobby."

"More than that, I'd say." I studied the pictures. "I mean, I don't know the first thing about photography, but these are amazing."

Nathan's face creased with a wide smile. "Thanks. Thanks, Cassidy."

I grinned back and glanced over at Felicia, who quickly covered her paper. Her desk was covered with pastels. "How about you, Felicia? Are you just about done?"

"I don't know," she said. She twisted her fingers in her thick tangle of curls. "I keep adding stuff and changing stuff and I can't tell if I'm making it better or wrecking it completely."

"Can I see it?" I asked.

Felicia shook her head. "You'll probably think it sucks."

"Nah, I've already taken first place in the suckage category. Sorry. You can't compete." I laughed. "Joe says he's making a glue stick sculpture."

"Seriously?"

"Until I took his glue sticks."

"Aha. Does that mean you've finally made something?"

"Mmm. Want to see it?"

Felicia stood up and followed me back to my desk. I lifted the papers I'd used to hide my art project. "See? Not art."

She stared at it. From a distance of a few feet, it looked like a mixed-up newspaper.

Victoria looked up from her own work. "Can I see?"

I nodded and she came and stood beside Felicia, bending down to look more closely.

In the end, I'd given up on painting and sculpture and finding images that called out to me. I'd decided that since I'd used all the art class time to write in my note-book, my notebook would have to be the raw material. So what I'd made was a collage of words and sentences and questions. A *Who is Cassidy Silver?* collage.

Victoria and Felicia stared and stared.

I squirmed. "Okay, I know it's not art."

Felicia finally turned to look at me. "That was brave of you," she said. "Letting us see that. Read that."

I met her eyes. "We're friends."

Felicia's cheeks were pink. "Yes," she said, "we are."

Victoria didn't meet my eyes, and I wondered what she was thinking. We hadn't talked about the telekin-esis thing since that day at the tobogganing hill, and I felt like it was kind of hanging between us. If she had made up the whole thing about her powers and Rick and all that—well, didn't that mean she didn't trust me with who she really was? And if she hadn't made it up, and I doubted her? Well, that wasn't right either.

"You want to see my picture?" Victoria asked.

I nodded. "Sure."

She flipped it around so we could see. "I had this idea in my head of how it should look, but I can't get it on to the paper," she said. "It's so frustrating."

She'd painted a face, which I guess was supposed to be hers—it had short brown hair and glasses—and crisscrossed it with lines, so that it looked like a jigsaw puzzle. The face was a bit too small for the paper, so there was a lot of empty white space around it, and one eye was a bit bigger than the other. That was exactly what happened when I tried to draw faces, and for some reason, that made me feel better.

"It's cool," I said. "It's a cool idea. You know, the puzzle thing."

Felicia nodded quickly. "Yeah, that's clever."

"You can just say it," Victoria said glumly. "I can't paint."

"I honestly do think it's a cool idea," I said. "And you paint better than I do. And at least you don't have a mother who's a famous artist."

She nodded, looking more cheerful. "Yeah, at least no one expects me to win the contest."

"Jeez. You don't think anyone expects me to, do you?" That hadn't occurred to me. I remembered Ms. Allyson saying she was a fan of my mother's work, and I hoped she wouldn't be disappointed when she saw what I'd done. Well, too late to do anything about that now.

I glanced at Victoria's picture again. A jigsaw puzzle. That was about right, I thought. I wasn't sure how all the pieces fit together, and it looked like maybe she wasn't quite sure either.

Twenty-one

I was standing at the bottom of the stairs waiting for Ben when Amber, Madeline and Chiaki came out of the school. I braced myself for the usual barrage of insults. Though, come to think of it, Amber had mostly been ignoring me lately.

Amber nodded at me.

I nodded back. A truce, maybe?

Then, wonder of wonders, Chiaki smiled at me. "Hi, Cassidy."

"Hi, Chiaki. How's it going?"

She glanced at Amber, a little nervously. "Okay."

"Come on, Chiaki. Let's go." Amber looped her arm through Chiaki's.

"Um. Okay. See you." Chiaki shrugged and followed Amber off across the schoolyard.

I stared after them. Wow. An almost friendly interaction. I wasn't sure what to make of it. I didn't want to hope for too much. If Chiaki wanted to be friendly, that was great. But if not, I'd survive. I had Victoria and Felicia and Nathan and maybe even Joe. Chiaki was welcome to join us, if she ever decided to climb way down the social ladder, but I didn't need my thumbuddy back anymore.

Ben came barreling through the doors, taking the steps two at a time. I nodded at him and we walked across the schoolyard together. "You okay?" I asked.

He nodded, stared at the ground and shuffled his feet through the snow. "Cassidy?"

"Yeah? What is it?"

"I'd rather just get it over with," he whispered.

I stared at him. "What are you talking about?"

"Tyler." His face was half covered by his wool scarf, and he looked up at me from behind fogged up lenses. "I know he's just waiting to get me alone."

"He won't get you alone." I felt uncomfortable as soon as the words were out of my mouth. Ben was right: If Tyler wanted to get Ben, sooner or later he would find a chance.

Ben just shook his head. He knew it too.

"My art show's coming up, you know," Mom told me and Ben over leftover Chinese food. "Next weekend. I was wondering if you two would be willing to help out."

I eyed her suspiciously. Those big canvasses weighed a ton and were really awkward to move. Usually Dad helped, but since he wasn't here…

Mom saw my expression and laughed. "Nothing too unpleasant. I've got friends helping with the setup, but Friday night is the opening and we're hoping for a good turn out. There'll be appetizers and drinks. I wondered if you two would like to help serve them."

"Like, walk around with trays of crackers and stuff?" I'd done that at one of her shows last year. "Sure, I don't mind."

"Can Sydney come too?" Ben asked.

"If he gets to invite Sydney, I want to invite Victoria," I added quickly. "And Felicia."

"One friend each. But if Sydney and Victoria want to come, I'd be more than happy to put them to work."

"Cool." I started planning my outfit. I'd seen a great hat in the window of the Sally Ann on my way home from school.

Mom interrupted my thoughts. "Invite them here for dinner on Friday. We can order pizza and then all go to the show together."

I made a face. "Mom? I honestly don't think I can face another pizza in this lifetime."

Ben's head bobbed up and down like it was on a spring. "Yeah, no more pizza."

"After this show is over, I won't be so busy." She frowned. "I'm sorry. I know I've been a bit distracted. With your dad away, I can't seem to stay on top of things."

Maybe if you didn't volunteer twenty hours a week and spend the rest of your time painting, I thought.

Then I felt bad. Selfish. Like I wanted her to abandon dying people so that I could have a lasagna. Or burgers. Or a stir-fry. Or a salad. My mouth watered. "Maybe if you volunteered a little bit less? Not quit or anything, but…"

"There's so much to do at hospice," she said. "I didn't intend to do so much, but the nurses are so busy and they keep asking me if I could just do one more thing."

Ben stood up abruptly. "Just say no, Mom."

I looked at him, startled.

"You're never here anymore," he said.

"I didn't know you felt like that." She turned and looked at me, her forehead wrinkled in an unspoken question.

I swallowed. "It's hard, Mom. When you're so busy, and everything you're doing is so important, it's hard to talk to you about stuff that seems less important."

"Less important?" She looked startled. "What are you talking about? Nothing is more important to me than the two of you."

Ben and I looked at each other. "It hasn't really felt like that," I said. "Not lately. Not since Dad left."

I turned to Mom and saw, with a shock, that her eyes were shiny with tears. "I'm sorry," I said, backtracking. I hadn't seen her cry for years, not since her father died when I was a little kid. "I mean, it's okay, we're okay."

She ignored me and started talking fast, like she just wanted to say whatever it was she had to say. "When your dad left on this contract, I couldn't stand it. I worried all the time. All those news stories about bombings and kidnappings."

"You said it was safe," I said, horrified.

"It is, it is. The area he's in is considered relatively safe, otherwise he wouldn't have gone." She rubbed her hands across her face. "But I couldn't stop worrying. I'd spend half the day on the Internet, scaring myself silly, waiting for the phone to ring. I couldn't go on like that. I decided I needed to keep myself busy somehow."

"Well, you sure managed that." I looked at her carefully. To my relief, the tears were gone and she looked a bit more like her usual self. "I guess you'll be pretty happy when Dad's home then."

She nodded. "Forty-seven days to go." Then she laughed. "Pathetic, huh? Missing him so much."

I thought of Victoria's parents and how they argued all the time. "No," I said, "it's not pathetic at all."

Twenty-two

On Friday, I handed in my art contest entry. On Saturday, I woke up with a stuffed up nose, a sore scratchy throat and a killer headache. I spent most of the weekend lying on the couch feeling lousy, and on Monday I was still too sick to go to school.

So Tyler finally got his chance.

Ben and Sydney burst through the front door after school. "Cassidy!" Ben shouted.

I'd been half asleep on the couch. I sat up. "What?" I croaked.

Ben came running into the living room, still wearing his winter boots and scattering lumps of ice across the carpet. "You won't believe this."

I stared at him. His hair was full of snow and his left eye was red and puffy, but he was grinning. "What happened?"

"Well, Sydney and I were walking home—"

I interrupted. "Mom told me she was going to pick you up."

"Yeah." Ben made a face. "I didn't want her to, so I told her that I'd be fine if I was with Sydney."

I sat up straighter and narrowed my eyes at him. "What about Tyler? What were you thinking?" I remembered what he'd said before. "You weren't just trying to get it over with, were you?"

He shook his head and started unzipping his jacket. Sydney appeared beside him, having already shed her boots and coat. Ben grinned at her and turned back to me. "We were walking along and all of a sudden this snowball whacked me in the side of the head. A real muddy icy one." He rubbed his reddened eye.

I winced, but Sydney was grinning so wide her smile practically split her face in two.

"You should have seen him," she said proudly. "He picked up a handful of snow, balled it up and whipped it right back at Tyler. Hit him smack in the face."

My eyebrows shot up. Ben is smart, but he can't throw a ball to save his life. "Seriously?"

"Total fluke," Ben admitted cheerfully. "It was perfect though. Tyler was yelling stuff at me and I guess he must have had his mouth open when the snowball hit him, because he started spluttering and coughing."

"Cool." I'm not usually the type to get excited about snowball fights, but I was nodding as proudly as Sydney. "Good for you, Ben."

"That's not all," Sydney said. "He told Tyler that this was it—that if he ever did anything to him again he was going to tell."

"And I told him that he should stop doing stuff like that. I told him he was going to develop an antisocial personality disorder and my mom could get his mother the name of a good child psychiatrist."

I started laughing. That sounded more like Ben.

"Anyway, he just stomped off," Ben said. He sounded amazed. "He just stomped off and left us alone."

"That's great," I said. "Good for you, Ben. I knew you could stand up to him." I felt a huge sense of relief. Maybe Tyler would leave him alone and maybe he wouldn't, but at least Ben was fighting back and feeling better. I'd wanted to solve this problem for him, but Sydney had been right. He'd had to do it himself.

I was back at school on Wednesday, red-nosed but generally recovered. Everyone was buzzing about the art contest. Ms. Allyson had said she would announce the winner at the end of the week. I knew it wouldn't be me, but I was still caught up in the excitement. It was hard not to be, the way everyone kept talking about it. Plus Victoria's words kept echoing in my head: *At least no one expects me to win.* Well, I hadn't even told Mom about the contest, so she wouldn't be disappointed, but I did feel like I was letting Ms. Allyson down. And it would have been so amazing to come home from school on Friday—the day of Mom's art show—and tell her that I'd won.

When Friday rolled around, the excitement in the classroom was electric. For once, everyone was sitting at their desks before the morning bell even rang.

Ms. Allyson walked in a couple of minutes late, wearing her red cowboy boots and a long black skirt. "Okay. I can tell no one is going to be able to concentrate or do any work until I announce the winner, right?"

We all nodded impatiently.

She gave a dramatic drumroll of her hands on the desk; then she laughed. "No, seriously, I want to say what a difficult decision this was. There were a few entries that were quite outstanding. It was very hard to choose only one to go on to represent the school. Personally, I wish I could have chosen several."

The suspense was killing me.

"The winner, who will be going on to represent our school at the district competition, is Felicia Morgan. Congratulations, Felicia!" Ms. Allyson smiled warmly. "Well done."

Felicia's round face was flushed. She looked very embarrassed but also very pleased. "Thank you," she said. Her voice was so soft I could hardly hear her.

"You deserve it," said Ms. Allyson. "Your work was wonderful." She held up Felicia's painting to the class.

I hadn't really seen it before; Felicia had been so shy about it. It was beautiful—much nicer than my mom's paintings, in my opinion. Dark green ferns swayed around disconnected images: whales, giant trees, strange birds. I could have looked at it all day. And I didn't even like art.

Our group had expanded: Victoria, Felicia, me, Nathan, Joe, two shy quiet girls called Tansy and Hannah, and a very smart, computer-obsessed guy called Ken. We had taken over a corner table in the lunchroom and were sitting around it, trading tuna sandwiches for peanut butter, and chocolate puddings for cookies.

Felicia was talking about her painting. "It's my memories of New Zealand," she said. "We left two years ago, but I still miss it. Someday I'll go back, to visit anyway." She looked at me. "I was worried you might be upset," she admitted. "I know how much you wanted to win."

"Nah, I knew I wouldn't win." I shrugged. "I'm over it."

"Do you want to be an artist?" Victoria asked Felicia.

"I'd love to. But I don't know how realistic that is. It's probably pretty hard to make enough money that way. I have an uncle in New Zealand who's an artist, but I never get to talk to him now."

I nodded. "You should talk to my mom some time. She's an artist."

"A really good one," Victoria said. She'd seen a bunch of Mom's paintings at our house. She looked around the table. "You guys should all come to the opening of her art show tonight."

"Oh, I wish I could," Felicia said.

"Can't you?"

"No, I have to babysit the little monsters that live next door."

I shrugged. "That's too bad. Well, come over after school sometime. Next week, maybe?" I had a feeling Mom might be home a bit more now.

Felicia smiled. "Thanks. I'd like that. Maybe your mom would show me some of her paintings."

Nathan looked interested. "Where is her show?"

"A gallery downtown. It's connected to that coffee shop—the Purple Pear."

Victoria nodded. "It's the coffee shop my mom works at."

I looked at her in surprise. "You never told me that. Will she be there tonight?"

"She'd better not be. She's not supposed to work tonight."

No one said anything. Victoria's face was closed off and her tone of voice didn't invite questions. Finally Joe started talking about something else, but I couldn't stop thinking about Victoria. Why didn't she want her mom to be there? Something was wrong, and I had no idea what it was.

"Cassidy, can you stay behind for a moment?" Ms. Allyson asked, just as the 3:20 bell sounded. She had to shout a little to be heard over the screeching of chairs and slamming of desks as everyone stampeded out of the room.

"Sure." My heart sank. It had to be about my not-an-art-project.

Ms. Allyson sat on the edge of her desk and crossed her legs. She met my eyes and laughed. "Don't look so worried."

I pulled my hat down more firmly on my head.

"Nice hat, by the way."

I stared at her and thought, Get on with it.

She cleared her throat. "I just wanted to have a quick word with you about your art project."

"You're disappointed, aren't you?" I tried to sound like it didn't bother me. "You hoped I'd be a painter, like my mom?"

"Not at all." She shook her head, like the idea had never crossed her mind.

"I know my project sucked. I mean, I guess it wasn't really art, right?" I screwed my mouth to one side. "Sorry. I don't think art's my thing."

She leaned toward me. "Maybe not painting, but your writing is wonderful. That's what I wanted to talk to you about. Your writing blew me away. Are you sure you're only twelve?"

"Last time I checked." My face was on fire. "Um. Thanks, Ms. Allyson."

"I mean it, Cassidy. You've got heaps of talent." She shook her head, and her long red curls swung slowly back and forth. "Keep writing."

I shrugged. "I think I'd kind of miss it if I stopped."

I was grinning like a fool as I left the classroom. I've always talked a lot—Mom says I was born talking and haven't stopped since—but who would have thought that putting all those words on paper would make me a writer?

Twenty-three

"Well, I didn't win the art contest," I blurted out as Victoria and I came through the front door.

Mom stepped into the front hall, looking surprised. "You never told me you'd entered one."

"Our whole class had to."

"Our friend Felicia won," Victoria explained. "I bet she'll come first at the district competition too and win the free art classes."

Mom was looking at me kind of funny. The house smelled like spices. "Did you make dinner?" I asked, changing the subject.

She took my arm. "Excuse us a moment, Victoria." She pulled me into the kitchen. A tray of homemade burritos sat steaming on the counter. "Now, would you please tell me what is wrong?"

I blinked furiously. For some stupid reason, I seemed to be crying. "I don't know," I said. My voice came out all choky.

Mom tilted her head to one side. "Honey, if you want the art lessons that badly, we can afford to pay for some classes for you. You've just never been interested before."

I shook my head. "I hate art," I wailed.

"Then what's wrong? Did something happen at school?"

"No, it's just, well, you…," I trailed off. I felt like an idiot, and Victoria was waiting in the front hall.

"What is it?"

"Mom, are you disappointed?" I blurted.

"Why would I be disappointed?"

I pushed the heels of my hands against my eyes and saw tiny red stars. My throat was aching, and I had to force the words out. "Because you're an artist."

She looked bewildered. "But that doesn't mean I want you to be one."

"It doesn't? You don't?"

"No, I mean, I don't mind if you are or not. I want you to be happy. I hope you and Ben both find something to do that you enjoy as much as I enjoy painting. I don't care if that is teaching, or acting, or—or bricklaying."

"Bricklaying?"

"You know what I mean." She shook her head slowly and smiled. "You funny thing."

"I ran in to your old teacher today," Mom said over dinner.

I'd almost forgotten about him. "McMoron? Ugh. I'm glad I wasn't there."

Victoria giggled. "Me too."

Mom frowned. "Have some compassion, would you? That poor man. Turns out he's the brother of a friend of mine."

"Poor man?" I stared at her. "Hello? Poor us, more like. He was awful."

She shook her head. "Well, he's had reason to be unhappy, that's for sure."

"What do you mean?"

"He had a terrible car accident a couple of years ago and his wife was killed. And it sounds like he's had chronic back pain since then too." She looked thoughtful. "That's probably why he was drinking."

"Mom! Does that mean it's true that he was drunk in class?"

She shook her head. "I shouldn't have said that. I don't really know. But anyway, it sounds like he's doing much better."

"I hope he's not coming back yet," I said. "I love Ms. Allyson."

"My mom used to drink a lot," Victoria said quietly. "When I was little."

"She did?"

"Yeah, but she quit years ago. She goes to meetings now. You know, AA."

I was kind of shocked, but Mom just nodded. "Good for her." Then she smiled. "Victoria, that reminds me. Your mother called this afternoon. She said to tell you her schedule got changed, so she'll be there tonight after all."

I glanced at Victoria. Her eyes were wide and shocked, and I remembered what she'd said in the lunchroom.

Mom wasn't looking at her. She was cutting up her burrito, still smiling. "I'm looking forward to meeting her," she said.

Victoria and I headed up to my bedroom to get changed while Ben and Sydney tried to finish a game of chess they'd started a couple of days ago. I wouldn't play chess with Ben because he took so long to make a move, but Sydney was just as bad as he was.

I rummaged through my closet. "Black and white outfits and no T-shirts with words on, Mom says." I blew a long disgusted raspberry. "You wouldn't think artists would be so uptight, would you? Aren't they supposed to be more, I don't know—"

"Relaxed?"

"Yeah." I pulled a long-sleeved, ruffled, white shirt off a hanger and held it up against myself in front of the mirror. "And, you know, Bohemian. What do you think of this shirt?"

"It's nice. I like the buttons on the sleeves."

"Hmmm." I tried on a black leather cap and took it off again. "So, how come you don't want your mom to be there tonight? You usually get along okay, right?"

She shrugged and didn't answer.

"I don't get it," I said. "What's the big deal?"

Victoria bit her lip and tucked her hair back tightly behind her ears. "I'd just rather she wasn't there, that's all." She picked at a loose thread in the cuff of her pants.

"There's more, isn't there? Something you aren't telling me?"

She looked down at her hand and started winding the thread around her finger. "She just doesn't understand anything. I can't tell her stuff because she'll just freak out."

"What kind of stuff?"

Victoria didn't answer.

I felt hopelessly out of my depth. "Are you sure you don't want to talk to my mom or someone about all this? Ms. Allyson? I bet you could talk to her."

She was shaking her head. "Don't tell anyone, Cassidy. You promised."

I held my hands up helplessly. "Okay. Okay. I won't say a word."

Twenty-four

We pulled our winter coats over our black-and-white outfits and piled into Mom's old station wagon. I sat in the front seat beside Mom. She'd put makeup on, and between that and the new hairdo, she looked all glamorous. I wished Dad was here to see her. In the backseat, Ben was squeezed between Victoria and Sydney, talking a mile a minute about some new kind of solar-powered car. I pressed my nose against the window, and my breath left a foggy circle on the cold glass.

Main Street was crazy busy. I walked down here pretty often in the daytime, but everything looked different after dark. Cars zipped by, throwing up a spray of slushy water, as Mom drove slowly past the gallery. All the parking spots right in front were already taken.

"Try Alma Street," I suggested.

Mom turned the station wagon onto a quiet residential street just past the gallery and squeezed into an empty spot between a blue pickup truck and a small red car.

We all got out and walked back around the corner to the gallery entrance. It was so cold, the inside of my nose crinkled with every breath I took.

I nudged Victoria. "Brrr."

She smiled, but her face stayed tense and anxious. I sighed. I still didn't know exactly what was wrong, but tonight wasn't going to be much fun unless Victoria lightened up a bit.

A purple sign in the shape of a pear and a mug blinked in the coffee shop window. Next door, the art gallery's front door displayed a poster advertising Mom's exhibit. I pushed open the door and stepped into the empty room: high ceiling, hardwood floor and Mom's paintings hanging on stark white walls. Mom ushered us through to the kitchen at the back. On the counter, large trays of tiny sandwiches, cut vegetables and dip, little cookies and squares were laid out.

"Good, the food's been delivered already." Mom looked at the four of us. "There are smaller trays there so take what you can carry and wander around."

"That's it?" Ben asked.

She frowned. "Say hello, be friendly, ask people if they would like anything to eat."

She looked nervous, I thought. She'd had lots of shows before, but I guess Dad was usually there to help with the details. "It all looks great," I told her. "We'll be fine."

"Thanks, Cassidy." Mom met my eyes and smiled. She pointed at a door on the other side of the counter.

"That's the coffee shop through there. It's a shared kitchen. They close in an hour and will be back here to put things away. Make sure you stay out of the way."

"It's just my mom," Victoria said.

Mom smiled. "That's right. I'll just pop through and introduce myself." She disappeared through the door, and I watched it close behind her.

"Come on," Ben said. "Let's get ready."

Victoria turned and started silently arranging tiny sandwiches on a tray. I opened my mouth to ask her what was wrong, then closed it again. Whatever was wrong, she obviously didn't want to talk to me about it.

By eight fifteen, Mom was pacing around, checking her watch every thirty seconds and complaining that it didn't look like anyone was going to show up. The rest of us stayed in the kitchen. Ben and Sydney goofed off, making up trays towering with cookies.

Ben's cookie tower tumbled and a couple of cookies fell on the floor and broke. "Smarten up, Ben," I hissed. "Just make up the tray properly. You won't be able to carry it if it's piled up like that."

He picked up the broken pieces and took a bite of one. "Mmm."

"It's more efficient to pile the food high," Sydney informed me earnestly. "Otherwise we'll have to keep coming back here to replenish our trays."

Replenish. I tried not to laugh. Sydney was so much like Ben.

Victoria ignored Sydney and made a face at Ben. "Gross," she said. "I wouldn't eat off the floor here. Mom says they have rats."

Ben's eyes widened and he opened his mouth to say something.

I wasn't in the mood for one of his long speeches about rats and the bubonic plague. "Come on, Victoria." I grabbed her arm. "Let's go. I think I hear people arriving."

A few more people trickled in, and then dozens arrived in a great rush. By eight thirty, the room was packed, the coatrack was overflowing and maneuvring through the crowds with the trays of food was an athletic feat. I kept catching snatches of conversation and couldn't resist eavesdropping. It felt funny to hear people talking about Mom's paintings.

A tall, skinny, blond woman with bright red lipstick was oohing and aahing over one of them. "It's absolutely perfect for the living room," she gushed.

Ugh. I didn't know how anyone could walk in heels that high. I tried to keep my face neutral as I approached, bearing my tray of sandwiches.

"Right above the couch, don't you think?" The woman turned to her companion. He was shorter than her, heavy and balding, with a jutting jaw and a face rather like a bullfrog. "Of course, we'd have to get rid of the rug. The colors would clash horribly. I saw a nice rug last week."

They were discussing the painting like it was nothing more than a decorating accessory. I felt a bit indignant on my mother's behalf, but I guessed if they were willing to spend the money, Mom wouldn't care why. I held out the tray. "May I offer you something to eat?"

The woman looked down at me like I was pond scum. "Certainly not," she said.

Whatever. I shrugged and turned away. Maybe I'd send Ben over with the plague cookies from the kitchen floor.

A gruff nasal voice spoke behind me. "Wait a minute there, waitress. Aren't you going to offer me anything to eat?"

Startled, I spun around. Bullfrog man.

"I'm sorry," I said politely, holding out my tray. "Would you like something?"

The man's hand hovered over the tray for a moment. A gold wedding ring was sunk into his fleshy finger.

"Arnold! You're not eating that sugary junk, are you? I thought you were on a diet." The blond woman tapped her foot impatiently.

The man pulled his hand back as if he'd been burned. He scowled at me. "No, no. Don't stand there like an idiot. I don't want anything."

Jerk. I backed away, my cheeks flaming, mentally reviewing what had just happened. Why was it that when someone acted like a complete idiot, I always felt like I must have done something wrong? I hated that. I gave bullfrog man a parting scowl, but he wasn't even looking my way.

I scanned the room, looking for Victoria, but couldn't see her. The room was packed. I pushed through a group of people, trying to get back to the kitchen, and felt someone grab my sleeve.

It was Ben, eyes wide behind his glasses. "You won't believe this," he said in a low voice.

I could hardly hear him over the noise of the crowd. "What?"

"Tyler is here! Isn't he the last person you would expect to see at an art show?"

"Are you sure?"

"Look over there," said Ben, nodding toward the back of the room.

I balanced my tray against my hip and followed his gaze. At the back of the room, leaning against the wall with a sulky look on his face, was Tyler Patterson.

"Huh. That is weird. You're not worried, are you?"

Ben grinned. "Nope." He squared his shoulders and flashed me a gap-toothed grin. "Last time he called me nerd-boy, I told him his epidermis was showing. And you know what he did? He checked his fly!" Ben took a bite of a cookie. "He didn't even know what it meant."

I raised my eyebrows, not sure I knew either. "Um, skin? You told him his skin was showing?"

He giggled through a mouthful of cookie. "Yeah, Sydney thought it was hilarious."

"Yeah, I bet she did." I leant back to avoid being sprayed with cookie crumbs. "I'm glad Tyler's backed off."

Ben stopped laughing abruptly. "You know, he actually looks a little nervous whenever he sees me. Funny how he really believed I'd call his mother, hey?"

"Wouldn't you?"

"Are you kidding?" He looked thoughtful. "Well, I guess maybe I would, if I had to."

"Good."

"Cassidy? You know what I said that one time, about it being your fault I got picked on?"

I remembered, all right. I nodded, concentrating on keeping my expression the same.

Ben looked uncomfortable. "I shouldn't have said that. And it wasn't true anyway."

"Really?"

"Yeah." He squirmed a little. "So, you know, I'm sorry."

"It's okay. I'm sorry about the stuff I said too. You know, you're fine the way you are." I grinned at him and punched his shoulder lightly. "Except for the part about your glasses. You shouldn't let Mom pick them for you."

Ben looked mildly offended. "I picked them myself."

I groaned. "Take me with you next time." I changed the subject. "Hey, listen, I can't find Victoria. Have you seen her?"

"She was over by the drinks table, serving cheese and crackers last time I saw her. But I haven't seen her for a while." Ben held up his almost empty tray in one hand. "I have to go re-stock. These people sure eat a lot." He disappeared through the door into the kitchen.

I followed him, added a few cookies to my tray and headed back into the crowd. It was insanely busy. Mom should be happy about the number of people who had come.

I scanned the room but still couldn't see Victoria. I felt increasingly uneasy. Then I saw a face I recognized.

Amber Patterson. Just what I needed.

Twenty-five

Amber was walking toward me, wearing a short black dress, shoes with heels and a tentative smile.

"Hi, Cassidy," she said.

"Hi, Amber." I held out the tray of cookies warily. Hopefully our truce was still in effect. "Would you like something to eat?"

Amber giggled. "I've already had about five." She looked over her shoulder guiltily. "My mother will kill me if she sees me."

"There's tons more in the kitchen. Eat as many as you want."

She took a chocolate cookie. "It must be fun, helping out here like this."

"It's okay."

"Your mom's art is real popular, isn't it? I don't think I understand it though. I like art that looks like something."

"I don't really understand it either," I admitted, starting to relax.

Amber took another cookie. "These are really good cookies anyway."

Over her shoulder, I spotted high heels woman and bullfrog man heading our way. Time for me to go. "I better get back to work," I told Amber.

The blond woman looked at Amber. "Poodle!" she cried. "What are you doing eating that junk?"

Amber looked mortified. "Mother!" she protested.

They were her parents? I felt a flicker of something I never expected to feel: sympathy for Amber Patterson.

"You listen to your mother, miss," said the man. "You're never going to be a model if you keep eating that garbage." He poked Amber in the belly—hard.

Amber squirmed away. "I don't care," she said sulkily. "Mom, Dad, this is Cassidy. She's Molly Silver's daughter."

Mr. and Mrs. Patterson's disapproving expressions were instantly replaced by big smiles. What a couple of phonies.

"Cassidy Silver!" Mrs. Patterson exclaimed. "How nice to meet you! Amber has told us so much about you."

"Yes, yes." Mr. Patterson nodded. He looked uncomfortable. I hoped he was feeling horribly embarrassed about how rude he'd been earlier.

"We just love your mother's work," Mrs. Patterson gushed. "We're just thrilled that you and Amber are such good friends."

I looked at Amber. Me and Amber, good friends? I opened my mouth but, for once, no words came out. Amber's eyes met mine with an expression somewhere between pleading and defiance.

I forced a smile. "Nice to meet you too," I said.

Ben and Sydney were in the kitchen. Their trays were piled high and ready to go, but they were sitting side by side on the counter, munching on vegetables and dip.

Ben looked up guiltily. "We're taking a little break," he mumbled, his mouth full of carrot.

"Whatever." I put my tray down on the counter. "Have you seen Victoria? I can't find her."

Ben frowned. "That's weird," he said. "Sydney and I thought we saw her come in here, but she must have left when we weren't looking, because when we came in the kitchen, she was gone."

"Her mother's working in the coffee shop, but I don't think she'd have gone to see her." I hesitated. I had a feeling that whatever was going on with Victoria, it wasn't something she wanted her mom to know about. "Ben? Would you pop your head in and check if Victoria's there?"

He nodded. "Sure. No problem."

A moment later he was back. "Is her mom the tall dark-haired lady with the glasses?"

That sounded about right. "Yeah, no sign of Victoria?"

He shook his head, frowning. "No, that's kind of weird, huh?"

I had this awful feeling that something was wrong. But I'd been feeling uneasy since we arrived. What was it? I shook my head hard, as if I could shake the answer loose.

An image popped into my mind. The dark street outside, the lights of Main Street reflected on its wet surface. The noise of our car tires in the slush as we pulled up to the curb around the corner from the gallery. The headlights of our station wagon lighting up the back of the small red car parked in front of us.

The small red car. I'd seen that car before. That day at school, hiding behind the Dumpster with Victoria. Rick's car.

I flew back through the crowds of people and out the front door. The street was cold, and in the sudden silence, my ears rang from the noise of music and laughter and conversation. I ran down the street, around the corner and onto Alma Street. There, just ahead of me, was our brown station wagon, and in front of it, the little red car. I stood there for a moment, my thoughts as thick and frozen as the slush soaking through my shoes.

If the car was still here, I reasoned, then Victoria was still here too, and everything was okay. It probably wasn't Rick's car at all. There must be hundreds of small red cars in town.

Then I heard voices coming from the alley behind the gallery. As quietly as I could, I made my way over there, keeping close to the buildings. The cold wind was blowing straight through my thin white shirt, and I wished I'd taken the time to grab my coat before running outside.

Just inside the mouth of the alley was a large metal Dumpster. I inched behind it. Hiding behind Dumpsters was becoming a habit. I waited, shivering and listening. I could hear low voices but couldn't make out any words. Jeez, it was cold. I wondered if I was being stupid. I mean, there wasn't really any reason to think that Victoria was in danger. For all I knew I was spying on some total strangers doing who-knows-what in a dark alley. Not smart.

I poked my head out an inch and caught my breath. Not total strangers. Victoria was standing maybe fifty feet away, arms folded across her chest. Rick towered over her, his face shadowed. It was pretty obvious from their body language that they were arguing. Rick raised his voice. "Come on," he said. "My car's just over here. Can we at least sit in the car to talk? I'm freezing."

Don't do it, I thought. I was between them and the car, but I couldn't see how I could stop them.

"I don't think so," Victoria retorted. "I agreed to meet you here because, well, I don't know why. Because you said you'd changed. But you haven't, have you?" She backed away from him slowly. "I'm not a little kid anymore, Rick."

"No, you're all grownup, aren't you? Little Miss Perfect."

"Rick, don't be like that."

"Too good to help me out. Too good to bend a few laws."

She stepped away from him. "I'm not eight years old anymore. If I helped you, and we got caught, we'd both be in trouble and you'd go to jail again." She shook her head. "Forget it, Rick. I'm going back to the gallery."

He grabbed her arm. "You're not going anywhere."

Twenty-Six

Rick hung onto Victoria's arm, ignoring her protests and half dragging her down the alley. My heart was racing. What if he kidnapped her or something? I wanted to run and get help, but if I came out from behind the Dumpster, Rick would see me. Maybe I could outrun him—he sure didn't look like an athlete—but he'd probably grab Victoria and be gone before I could get back.

Come on, Victoria. Do something, I thought. If she was really telekinetic, why wouldn't she make something fall on his head or trip him? I wished I had a way to let her know I was watching. They were getting closer, and I could see that Victoria's face was streaked with tears and her eyes were wide and scared. Maybe she was too frightened to use her powers?

If only I could lift up that box of garbage over there. I imagined lifting it into the air and dropping it on Rick's head. I stared at it, unblinking, until my eyes stung and watered.

It didn't move. Newsflash: I wasn't going to be a superhero.

I peeked out again. They were level with my Dumpster, heading down the alley toward Alma Street.

"You owe me, Victoria," Rick yelled. "These guys are going to kill me if I don't pay them back. You're the only one who can help me."

"What are you talking about?" Victoria sounded furious. "It's got nothing to do with me. You keep showing up and wrecking everything."

Rick's face was screwed up with anger. "Oh, I'm wrecking your life, am I? Well maybe that's your karma, because you sure wrecked mine. You showed up and all of a sudden, Dad had no time for me anymore. It was all about his baby girl."

"That's not fair. I can't help what happened when I was born. It's not my fault Dad left your mom."

"You and your stupid alcoholic mother."

Something clicked in my head. Name calling. Threats. Amber. Tyler. Rick was older and bigger and tougher, but what was he? Just another bully.

"She isn't drinking," Victoria said quietly. "Not anymore."

"Oh? So everything is hunky-dory now, is it? Just one happy family now that you've gotten rid of me?"

She shook her head. "No, if you really want to know, it isn't that great."

"Doesn't matter," Rick said. "What matters is that

I've found you now, and you're going to help me make some serious cash."

"Rick, I'm not...I can't do it," Victoria whispered. "I can't help you like that."

My palms were slick with sweat and my heart was pounding. Rick might be just a bully, but I had to admit it: He scared me. I heard myself coaching Ben, that day on the toboggan hill. You have to make him think he doesn't scare you, I'd told him. What had I learned from being bullied? How to act. It was all about acting.

I took a deep breath, clenched my fists and stepped out of the shadows. "Rick!"

He spun around, dragging Victoria with him.

"You're wasting your time," I said, trying to hold my voice steady and doing my best to seem bored and unconcerned. "She can't do that weird stuff anymore. She's a big fake."

Victoria stared at me. I couldn't tell what she was thinking. She drew in a long shaky breath; then she started to cry. "She's right, Rick. I really can't."

Rick didn't let go of her arm. "Don't give me that crap, Vicky. Remember how much fun we used to have?"

"Not for me. It wasn't fun for me."

"It was. You loved it. You used to beg me to take you out. You thought it was great."

She shook her head. "I thought *you* were great."

Rick stared right through her. "Not anymore, huh?"

"No." She looked down at the ground. "Not so much anymore."

"Look," I told him, "let her go. Maybe she had some strange powers back when you guys were kids, but she sure doesn't now."

Rick gave an unpleasant snorting laugh. "Maybe? You think I imagined all that?" He frowned. "Look, I'm not crazy. I may have some problems, but I know what happened. I know what she can do."

"If she could really do that stuff, don't you think she'd be doing it now?" I asked, trying to keep my voice calm. Maybe if I kept Victoria calm and gave her some ideas, she'd be able to use her powers to get rid of Rick. "Go on, Victoria. There's a whole Dumpster full of garbage right here. Why don't you pick it up and dump it on him?"

There was a long silence. Victoria and Rick were both looking back and forth from me, to the Dumpster, to each other. I held my breath. Come on, Victoria.

Victoria stared at the Dumpster. Nothing happened.

I turned my hands palm up at my sides in an exaggerated gesture. "See? I told you. She can't do it." I turned to Victoria. "We'd better get back inside. I told the others I'd only be a minute."

"Mom would kill me if she knew I agreed to meet you," Victoria told Rick. "You better get out of here."

"Don't talk to me about your mother." His face hardened. "How do I know you're not just lying to me?

Maybe you can still do that crazy stuff, and you just don't want to help me out."

"Get lost, Rick." Victoria tried to yank her arm free, but Rick still didn't let go. She started yelling, tears running down her face. "I used to be crazy about you, you know that? I was so stupid. I was actually happy that you called me. But you just wanted to use me, didn't you? You've never cared about me at all."

My stomach tightened. I'd been using her too, at first—trying to make her teach me telekinesis, pushing her to help Ben. I raised my voice. "Leave her alone!"

"Mind your own business," he snapped. "Stupid kid."

Maybe I couldn't use telekinesis to pick up a box of garbage but there was nothing wrong with my arms. I walked the few steps toward it, picked it up and heaved it in Rick's direction. It landed a couple of feet away from him—rotten vegetables, old clothes, empty packages and tin cans flew everywhere.

"Whoa, whoa." Rick stepped backward, finally letting go of Victoria's arm. "Jeez, kid, are you crazy?"

There was a long silence. We all stood there, staring at each other and at the garbage strewn all around us.

"Look, I get the point, okay? Fine. I can't make you help me." He rattled off a string of swear words. "I just can't believe this. I've been counting on you, Vic. Seriously. I'm up the creek if I don't come up with some cash."

"I'm sorry. If I had any money, I'd give it to you." Victoria covered her face with her hands, but I could tell she was still crying.

My heart was hammering away like crazy. "Maybe you should just leave town," I suggested. "Leave town and leave Victoria alone. Because if anything happens to her, I'll know exactly who's responsible. And believe me, your family may keep bailing you out, but I'd have no problem going straight to the cops." I winced. *Thraight to the copth.*

Rick didn't seem to notice. He ran his hands over his shaved head and looked a bit lost, like he had no idea how he ended up in this situation and no clue what to do or say next.

Victoria looked up at him and wiped her eyes. "Maybe you could get some help," she whispered.

"You think I haven't tried that a hundred times before?" He looked down at Victoria, and I thought I saw his face soften a tiny bit. "This is for real, Vicky? You can't do those things anymore?"

"For real," she said, sniffing.

Rick held her eyes for a long moment, like he was trying to figure out if she was telling him the truth. Finally he shrugged. "I guess it doesn't matter whether you can't help me or you won't help me."

Victoria looked at him and her voice was almost a whisper. "I have to go."

"Okay, whatever. Go then." He hesitated and then,

just as we turned to leave, he called her name. "Victoria! Look, what you said about me not caring about you… you know that's not true, don't you?"

She shrugged. "That's how it feels."

Rick kicked at an empty bottle and swore under his breath. "Nah. That's not right." I watched the emotions flicker across his face and for the first time I thought I caught a glimpse of the big brother Victoria used to be so crazy about. Maybe even still was.

He hesitated for a second, like he might say something more, but then he just turned and stomped away without looking back.

Back inside the gallery, everyone was still milling around looking at Mom's paintings. I pulled Victoria into the empty kitchen and we sat shivering side by side on the floor.

"I'm sorry," she whispered. "He said he just wanted to talk. I didn't think he'd try anything like that."

I leaned forward, trying to see her face, but she was staring down at the floor. "Are you okay?"

"Not really."

"You know I was bluffing about you being a fake," I told her quickly. "I just thought if we could make him believe it, maybe he'd leave you alone."

She looked up at me, teary-eyed. "Does that mean you do believe me? That I'm really telekinetic?"

I hesitated. "I wasn't sure, at first. I wanted it to be true, but it's pretty hard to believe, you know?" I tried to read her expression, to gauge if she was mad at me. "To be honest, I did wonder if you might be making it all up. But I kind of decided it didn't matter if you could do it. I wanted to be friends either way."

"I can't do it," she whispered, not looking at me. "When I was trying to teach you, I tried at home a couple of times, with small things, and I couldn't do it. Nothing happened."

I remembered all the hours I'd spent staring at imaginary green energy. "So you've just been laughing at me all along? Thinking it would be funny to make me believe it?"

"No! I wasn't laughing. I wanted to tell you the truth. I just couldn't, somehow." She shook her head miserably. "Cassidy? I don't want you to be mad at me. And I really did think you might be able to learn to do it yourself."

"I'm not mad exactly. Mostly confused. I mean, if you aren't telekinetic, why was Rick trying to…why did he…?"

"Oh, I really could do stuff when I was younger. But it caused so much trouble with Rick and everything that I stopped doing it. Even then, sometimes, if I got mad or upset, things just happened and I didn't have control over them. It was scary."

"So that part was true then?" I felt a little better, somehow, knowing it hadn't all been lies. "Why do you think it stopped working?"

She shook her head. "I don't know. Maybe because I didn't want it to work, or maybe because I didn't practice? Or maybe just because I'm older." She twisted a short lock of hair around her finger. "I shouldn't have let you go on thinking I could do it."

"No, you shouldn't." I sucked on my bottom lip and tried to be fair. "Though I guess me being so excited about it probably didn't make it any easier for you to tell me."

She nodded gratefully. "Yeah, I really wanted to be friends."

"Yeah, well, me too, but not only because of that." I thought of something else. "Wait a minute though. That day in class, a few weeks ago, with Mr. McMaran?"

"I don't know. I've thought and thought about it."

I remembered the expression on her face—the reason I had suspected she was doing something in the first place. Magic, I'd thought. "You looked like you were concentrating so hard."

"I was so angry. I was trying to make something happen. The way I used to be able to when I was younger."

"So did you?"

"Honestly, I don't know exactly." She sighed. "I thought I did, maybe. I mean, I got mad and then all that stuff happened. But I guess I just wanted to believe I could still do it." She looked at me and made a face. "I couldn't have written that stuff on the board. I'm awful at math."

"I did wonder about that," I admitted, starting to laugh.

She giggled. "I guess it is sort of funny." Then she turned serious again. "The last time I did anything, you know, unusual, was over a year ago. Before we moved here. Since then, nothing at all. Believe me, I've tried. I really can't do it anymore."

I stopped laughing and looked sideways at her. "Do you mind much?"

"No." She made a face. "Not too much, anyway. It's kind of a relief."

I sighed. "I still think it would be amazing, being able to do something like that."

"Cassidy?" Victoria's breath caught. "Do you mind a lot? That I can't do it, I mean?"

"Just that you lied to me," I said. "I was going crazy, trying to figure out whether you were really telekinetic, and trying to learn it myself, and feeling guilty that I doubted you sometimes."

There was a long silence. Victoria's cheeks were pink and her eyes were teary. "I'm sorry," she whispered. "I don't know why I did. I guess being telekinetic has always been this really big part of who I am and when it stopped working, well, I sort of didn't know who I was anymore."

"I would have liked you anyway."

She ignored me. "And then you suspected that I'd done something magic…"

"Yeah."

Victoria's voice was so low I had to strain to hear her. "I wanted us to be friends. I wanted you to think I was special."

I swallowed. There was a lump in my throat. "Newsflash," I said gruffly. "You *are* special."

Just then, the door to the coffee shop opened and Victoria's mother stepped in.

"Victoria? Are you okay? I've been looking for you everywhere."

Victoria scrambled to her feet. "I know, I heard you call us. I should have told you but I—"

Her mother looked pale and worried, the dark frames of her glasses standing out against her skin. "Are you all right? You look like you've been crying."

She nodded slowly. "Yeah, well, there are some things I have to tell you."

Her mom raised her eyebrows. "I guess there must be."

"I'll see you at school," Victoria told me. "Tell your mom I'm sorry I couldn't stay for the whole show." Then she took her mom's hand, and the two of them disappeared through the door into the coffee shop.

Twenty-Seven

Finally the last few people straggled out the doors, and the gallery was empty and quiet.

"Right," Mom said. "I've kept you kids up well past your bedtime. Let's go home and hit the sack." She glanced around. "Is Victoria in the kitchen?"

Explanation time. "She's gone home with her mother," I said. I looked up at her and my stomach tightened. "Mom? There's some things I want to tell you." I looked at Ben and Sydney, who were yawning widely and rubbing their eyes. "A lot of things. But it can wait until tomorrow." I frowned. "If you have time?"

Mom smiled and stroked my hair ever so softly. "Honey...I've got all day."

I figured we might need it.

Victoria and I played phone tag on the weekend but didn't end up talking until Monday morning. I saw her heading across the schoolyard and ran over to meet her.

"So? How did it go with your mom? Did you tell her about meeting Rick?"

She grinned; then she cocked her head to one side and looked thoughtful. "She was nowhere near as mad as I thought she'd be. And she told my dad everything and they didn't fight about it." She shrugged. "So that's good, I guess."

"Tell me you're not grounded for life."

She shook her head. "It was stupid of me to agree to meet Rick there, but it turned out to be a good thing. He knows I'm not going to help him, so I don't think he'll come after me anymore."

It was the answer I'd been hoping for, but she didn't look happy. "Are you okay?" I asked. "Aren't you relieved that it's over?"

She nodded; then she sighed. "It's just sad, you know? He's so screwed up."

I remembered that brief moment in the alley when Rick suddenly went from looking scary to looking lost, and I thought of that photograph in Victoria's dining room of the smiling freckled-faced boy. It was sad, really sad, and there was nothing I could say that would change that.

Ms. Allyson looked more serious than usual when we all filed into the classroom that morning. She waited for the screeching and scraping of desks to stop and the chatter to die down before she spoke.

"This will be my last week with you all," she said. "Mr. McMaran will be returning next Monday."

My heart sank, and the classroom erupted in a chorus of protests. Joe Cicarelli raised his hand and spoke without waiting to be called on. "No offence," he said, "but that sucks."

Joe was wearing a new T-shirt. It read, *Work is for Mortals.* He looked up as I was reading it and winked at me. "Nice shirt," I mouthed, and he grinned back.

Ms. Allyson shook her head. Maybe it was my imagination, but her curls didn't seem to have their usual bounce and her eyes looked a bit shinier than they should. "I'm sad about it too," she admitted. "You've been a great class, and I've enjoyed being here. But give Mr. McMaran a chance. You might be surprised."

I remembered what Mom had said about his wife dying in a car accident and how he was in pain all the time. It was strange: it didn't make me like him any more, and it certainly didn't make him a better teacher, but it did make him seem more like a real person. Kind of like meeting Amber's parents. I knew I'd think about them whenever I saw Amber or Tyler. It was a lot harder to hate people when you knew more about them.

I wondered if Mr. McMaran would take all the pictures down again. Maybe if we all stuck together as a class, he'd listen to us. Then again, maybe not.

All I knew was that sometimes things didn't turn out the way you expected. A few weeks ago, I was Cathidy Thilver, school freak with no friends. And now look at me: If I made any more friends, I wouldn't have enough fingers to count them on.

On Friday, Victoria showed up at school with a huge grin on her face.

I looked at her glumly. "Quit smiling. It's a day of mourning here at Parkside." I'd worn all black: black jeans and a black jacket over a plain black T-shirt. No words, out of respect for the sadness of the occasion. I'd brought my *Nobody Knows I'm Elvis* shirt as a good-bye gift for Ms. Allyson. I figured she would appreciate it.

I made a face at Victoria. "It's the last day of freedom and learning and—"

"Hush," she said, giggling. "Guess what?"

"What?"

She reached into her jacket pocket and pulled something out.

"A postcard?"

"From Rick." She handed it to me. "From Vancouver. He's moved out west."

I took the postcard from her: A bunch of orca whales jumping out of the water with snowy mountains in the background. I flipped it over and read out loud: "Dear Vicky, Sorry if I upset you the other day. Decided your smart-mouthed friend was right and it was time for a fresh start. Wish me luck, Rick."

She was nodding and smiling.

"Your smart-mouthed friend?" I repeated. "He called me smart-mouthed?"

"Isn't it great though? I hope he really can get a fresh start out there."

"Me too," I said. I meant it, but I wasn't going to hold my breath waiting for him to get it together. Mostly I was just glad that he was two thousand miles away.

When the bell rang at three twenty, I hung back.

Ms. Allyson stood beside her desk, smiling. "Cassidy."

All of sudden I felt kind of stupid. She wouldn't want my old T-shirt. I fumbled in my briefcase anyway and pulled it out, neatly folded and in a plastic bag. "It's my Elvis shirt. I thought maybe you might like to have it." I shrugged, embarrassed. "It's clean. I mean, I washed it and everything." Duh.

Her face lit up. "Really? Are you sure?" She walked over to me, took the bag, pulled the T-shirt out and held it up against herself. "I love it. And it'll fit too. Thank you so much."

"No problem." I hesitated. "It's been really nice having you as a teacher."

She smiled. "I meant every word I said about your writing, you know. I hope you'll keep it up."

I nodded. "I will."

"Good."

"Well, I guess I'll see you around," I said, taking a step backward.

"Wait a minute." She opened her desk drawer. "I have something for you too."

I blushed. "Um, you don't have to give me something just because I gave you an old T-shirt."

"No, no. I know that. Hold on a sec." She pulled out a book. "I want you to have this."

I held out my hand and took it. It was a red leather notebook filled with lined pages. "For me to write in?"

She nodded. "Yes. Exactly."

Outside, the sun was shining. The temperature had crept up above zero and was hovering there. The snow was melting, and I could hear the dripping and tinkling of water running into the gutters. I sat down on the bottom step, opened the notebook and traced the faint blue lines with my fingertip. The book was so beautiful it was hard to bring myself to write in it. I didn't know where to start. I sat there for a moment, feeling the sun's warmth on my face. Then I started writing. I began in the same place I'd begun before. *Who is Cassidy Silver?* I studied the words for a moment, and then I grinned. *I am,* I wrote. *I am Cassidy Silver.*

Robin Stevenson grew up in England and Ontario, and now lives in Victoria, BC. She is the author of several other novels for children and teens, including *Out of Order, Dead In the Water* and *Big Guy*. More information about Robin is available on her website: www.robinstevenson.com.